HIS  PIECE

THE PREQUEL

MERRICK & JOCELYN

BY NICKI GRACE

STARRING:

Merrick Alexander & Jocelyn Milner

GUEST APPEARANCE:

Ashton Kent & Jada Scott from
HIS MOUTHPIECE: ASHTON & JADA

Raquel Ash from **THE LOVE IS SERIES**

Playlist

This playlist was not created to match with specific chapters. It is simply what I played on a loop while writing this book and I wanted to share it with you. Enjoy!

Everyday - Ariana Grande
Dangerous Woman - Ariana Grande
If you Let Me - Sinead Harnett
Under the Influence - Chris Brown
Go Fuck Yourself - Two Feet
Feel It - Michele Morrone
Seduction - Usher
Living Room Flow - Jhené Aiko
Positions - Ariana Grande
En Vogue - Don't Let Go
Neyo - Say It

Positions

*Here's a list of adventurous bondage positions you should try.
Some of them were even used in this story.*

*Overworked
Eiffel Tower
Chair Bondage
The Wheelbarrow
Spreader Bar Legs
Sword Crab Tie
Spread Eagle
Bottom's Up*

A Sexy Warning

THIS NOVEL IS FICTION.

It is a beautiful **Dom/sub** love story that contains **explicit** and **graphic scenes/sexual content such as; name-calling, bondage, forced orgasm, rough sex, edging and other wild stuff that I have heard of.**

Now, if you are not into all that, I still want you to stay and enjoy the story. You can be part of the wallflower community, and I promise **I won't pressure you** to participate in any way, although **my characters might.**
But if you're adventurous and simply must try everything you read, then you are the reason **I'm giving this disclaimer.**

While some of these positions may sound exciting, and trust me, they are, do so **at your own risk.**

In my personal opinion, if you don't stretch regularly, **are not a professional gymnast, or you're beyond a certain age, don't play <u>SUPERWOMAN</u>.** Paramedics rushing in at 2 am to bend your naked body back into its intended shape is sexy for no one.

You're welcome.

Now that all the warnings have been given, let's get to the excitement. **Grab some wine, all your toys, plungers, cucumbers, and all the dicks (*real and fake*), and let's get started.**

Chapter One

"FACE THE
HEADBOARD."

The first guy slides his dick into my mouth a moment before the second guy plows himself deep into my pussy from behind. The force of it causes the guy I'm sucking to get some premature deep-throat action... and I fucking loved it.

I locked my lips tight around his erection, then bobbed my head up and down a few times before glancing up to lock eyes with him. He was attractive, no correction, he was breathtakingly handsome, which is one reason why I wanted to sleep with him and his friend.

I think their names were Merrick and Xavier, although I couldn't be sure because my focus was on how sexually enticing they both were.

Neither of them knew my name and that was the way I preferred to keep it. No strings, no awkward conversations, and no plans of ever seeing either of them again.

Xavier, the one pounding the life out of me from behind, was a professional hockey player who lived in Canada.

He was over six feet tall, with golden brown skin and wide shoulders that suited his athletic build. He was clean-shaven and also very attractive, but due to his underwhelming stroke game, my attraction to him stopped at the physical.

It appeared all the time Xavier spent on the ice was spilling over into his sex moves. He was knocking his dick around like a hockey stick, trying to locate my puck and not having much luck.

It didn't necessarily feel bad, just as if he wasn't spending enough time on my most sensitive areas. Fortunately for me, the thrill of giving in to such a scandalous evening gave me the rush I sought.

Merrick, the one currently occupying my mouth and oddly enough, calming my mind, was the businessman. He was probably 6"2, with a muscular build and chocolate skin so captivating I found myself working extra hard to get him to his climax.

His dick was magnificent, and I anticipated the treat would be very sweet when he came.

I'd met them less than an hour ago at the hotel's bar downstairs. The attraction both men had for me was evident, but I didn't want one, I wanted them both.

Initially, I don't think either was too thrilled with the idea of sharing. They would have preferred if I chose one of them as the lucky guy that had me all to himself.

However, once I revealed that it was a fantasy of mine to have a threesome and that I wasn't wearing any underwear, they put their reservations aside, and here I was, forming a bridge between the two of them.

Xavier was on the bed, driving into me from the rear, I was in the middle, and Merrick was standing at the foot of the bed, his dick aligned perfectly with my mouth.

Xavier's thrusts were causing my body to lurch back and forth so fast that I had to take a break from sucking. I pulled Merrick's dick from my mouth and worked my hand up and down his shaft.

It was rock hard, thick, and stretched longer than the seven inches I was used to working with from my ex, Aaron.

Merrick twisted his fingers into my hair just the way I liked it, and I vaguely wondered if it would be rude to ask Xavier to leave when he was done since I was vibing way too much with his friend.

Something about him made me feel engaged and free all at the same time. After the day I'd had, his aura was exactly what I needed.

"I know you aren't getting tired on me are you, beautiful?" Merrick said.

Oh. My. Damn.

His voice was euphonious! It was deep, sensual and soothing. It vibrated through me and delivered a controlled yet peaceful vibe that put my body at ease.

A needy moan escaped my lips as I gradually swept my tongue over the length of him.

"I could never get tired when the dick tastes as good as yours," I responded, glancing up at him.

He smiled down at me, a pleased expression on his face.

"In that case, put your hands behind your back so that I can make sure you taste all of it."

"Whatever you say," I replied with a flirty grin.

After kissing the tip, I released him and placed my hands behind my back. Immediately Xavier gripped my wrists with one of his hands and held them in place. He used his other hand to reposition my waist before his relentless pounding resumed.

"Fuuuckkk, your pussy feels so good," Xavier grunted. I tossed my ass back a few times, maximizing his efforts and feeling a new spike in pleasurable sensations of my own.

Then, I opened wide and stuck out my tongue, allowing Merrick to coax his dick into my mouth, stretching my lips further and further apart with each inch. He put one leg on the bed, tightened his hold on my head, and began slipping that tasty dick in and out of my mouth.

My shoulders relaxed, and my lips tightened around his

member. I loved sucking dick, and I knew how to suppress my gag reflex, which meant he could fuck my mouth all night if he wanted to.

"That's it whore, suck that cum right out of my dick," Merrick said with a relaxed sigh as he pumped his hips.

His actions, accompanied by the use of such a dirty word jabbed into me. No guy had ever called me a whore before, and shit... I think I liked it. It fueled something within me and I found myself sucking so hard you would have thought I was trying to leave a hickey.

I hummed hungrily on his manhood, my need to please him increasing with each moan that escaped his lips.

Xavier suddenly found my spot again, and the realization that I had two men using me to get off magnified my arousal.

I could tell they both were closing in on their climax, but the only man I cared about was the one I faced. I wanted him to cum so badly that it almost felt like my orgasm was intertwined with his.

"Shit!" Xavier suddenly exclaimed.

He jerked hard and dug his fingers into my lower back as he came. The pressure prompted me to respond and I wiggled my ass and twirled my tongue faster, trying to keep up with the needs of both men.

It wasn't long before Xavier went slack, breaking his grip on my wrists. He withdrew from me, and now I was free to use my hands again... perfect.

Merrick was still holding on strong, but not for long. I grabbed his ass and pulled him as deep into my mouth as possible, swallowing several times. The technique caused my throat to contract around him repeatedly, and a few seconds later, his thick, warm release spilled down my throat.

When he was done, Merrick stepped back and stared down at me, his chest heaving.

"A woman that enjoys pleasing," he said. "If I am not mistaken, I do believe you enjoyed that just as much as I did."

Getting up on my knees, I licked my lips slowly before blowing him a kiss. "Oh, I definitely enjoyed it more than you."

The way he looked at me was animalistic. Equally dangerous and enthralling, compelling me to hold his gaze. He bit his lower lip, revealing perfect white teeth, then slowly released it, making my aching center quake.

I slid my hand down my stomach and between my thighs to massage my swollen clit. I still hadn't come yet, so I was ready for more action.

"I got it from here," Merrick suddenly said to Xavier without taking his eyes off me.

His tone was direct and unapologetic. I turned to look at Xavier. He was still naked, standing over the trashcan, about to drop the used condom inside.

Xavier smirked, and a knowing look passed between the two men while feelings of irritation ignited in me.

What the hell is going on? I wondered.

"Sure thing," Xavier said.

Without another word, he got dressed and gave me a wink before leaving the room.

"What the hell was that?!" I exclaimed once Xavier left. I was feigning annoyance because truth be told, I didn't care that Xavier was gone, but I didn't want Merrick to know that. "You can't just end my threesome. I asked for both of you, not just one."

Merrick placed one knee on the bed and slowly climbed in towards me and I began to back up. I wasn't sure why, but something about his gaze told me this was about to get real serious.

"Beautiful, I already told you, sharing isn't my thing. And

if you wanted him to stay, you would have objected before he left."

I continued to pretend like the fact that this man was coming toward me with only one goal in mind didn't thrill me to my very core.

As I moved back, Merrick drew closer. He was so enticing, with all his muscles, vigor and extraordinary good looks. He smiled at me, displaying two deep dimples that increased my weakness for him. The tension between us was so magnetic that I had no idea how to handle this situation.

What was my next move here? Make a snappy comeback? Yank him to me for a kiss?

Normally, I could hold my own and take what I wanted from men, but this man was something totally different. I could feel it.

Deciding to utilize my nonchalant attitude, hoping it would make me appear more in control and fearless, I said, "Who cares what your thing is. And if you don't like sharing, you did a great job doing it for the first half of the night."

My smart-aleck response didn't phase him in the least.

"That was before I liked you," he said.

I glanced down, his dick was still hard and it made my mouth water and my pussy pulsate.

Rolling my eyes, I curtly said, "Do you make a habit of sleeping with women you don't like?"

"Do you make it a habit of fucking men you don't know?" he retorted casually.

I opened my mouth to respond, but nothing came out. Merrick stopped moving. He was now fully facing me, and I was back as far as I could go, halted by the headboard and a large euro pillow cushioning my back.

Merrick cocked a brow. "Are you done debating with me?"

"Maybe," I said, crossing my arms. My nipples were hard as shit. "Why?"

"Because I noticed you haven't cum yet. Do us both a favor and stop talking so I can remedy that for you."

I wanted to curse him out, but he looked so scrumptious that even in my annoyance I craved more of what he was offering.

"Are you sure you can take care of it? Maybe you need some help to handle a woman like me."

Merrick's eyes narrowed and his expression became unreadable.

"Face the headboard," he ordered with a nod.

"Why?" I asked.

His lips lifted at the corners. "Trust me, you're going to need something to hold on to."

Some guys talked a big game. As if they were high achievers when they were actually losers, boosting themselves up. Well, Merrick wasn't all talk; he was a winner, and tonight, he would take home the championship trophy.

I should have known by the way he entered me that I was in trouble. He used two fingers to massage my pussy and stretch it open before sheathing his spasm-inducing dick into me.

From there, I was at a loss, not just for words, but for how to contain myself.

When he said I would need something to hold on to, he wasn't kidding. If I let go of this headboard, I wasn't certain that my soul wouldn't leave my body.

Waves of arousing sensations held me captive as they vibrated through me. Thrust after orgasmic-building thrust forced me further out of my reality into a world I had never experienced.

Who is he? And how is he doing this?!

I clutched, clawed, and damn near climbed that headboard as my impending climax began to stir within me, threatening to shatter me from the inside out.

"Do you still taste my cum on your tongue?" he suddenly asked.

His voice was so deep and demanding it sent shivers through me.

"Yes... Yes... I do," I cried out.

"Good. I want you to savor that taste and never forget how much you enjoyed being my whore tonight."

His dirty talk was undoubtedly drawing my orgasm to the surface.

"I won't," I promised.

Wrapping one large hand around my waist and using the other to flatten my upper body against the bed. I was forced to release the headboard and find a new anchor – the edges of the mattress.

I wanted to participate and keep up with his thrusts, but none of that was possible. He was driving this vehicle. I was merely along for the ride.

There was hair pulling and nail biting– both things done by me, to me.

It sounded dramatic, but I had no idea if I was coming or going. I just needed to catch a grip of something... anything, and Merrick was not making that easy.

He lifted my waist, digging his dick deep into me as his experienced hands explored my body, toyed with and squeezed my nipples, caressed my abdomen, and applied pressure, not just on, but around my clitoris.

I swore, I screamed and I just knew things couldn't get any more intense.

But when he leaned close and whispered, "cum for me," it felt like a dam broke and my orgasm was so powerful I momentarily blacked out.

Everything went dark and all sound ceased as my body surrendered to his command. I was floating and shaking, with my fingers locked around the sheet so tight I tore it from the corners of the bed.

"What... the... fuck," I said, breathing so hard I could barely get the words out.

I wasn't sure if it were a question, a statement, or an inner thought I'd accidentally shared out loud.

"You did good," Merrick said, pulling out of me.

"Huh?" I said, trying to roll over. My weak limbs still weren't functioning properly.

"I said you did good. You lasted longer than I expected."

"Uh huh," was all I managed to say.

What did that even mean? Was he timing this?

It felt like he was talking in circles, and I was too exhausted to keep up.

Vaguely, I wondered if he orgasmed this time, but ultimately, I decided that it wasn't my problem. If he didn't cum, that was his loss. I was satisfied, which meant it was time to go.

Merrick tossed his condom into the trash and walked over to my side of the bed.

"Need some help sitting up?" he asked with a smirk.

"No, I'm good," I replied, cutting my eyes at him. He was so smug.

It took me three attempts to finally sit up. The whole time Merrick watched me with that damn arrogant grin on his gorgeous face. We both knew he'd just owned my ass.

Thankfully, he let me get myself together without making any further comments so that I could at least leave with some dignity.

"You're welcome to stay if you'd like," he offered, getting back into the bed.

I was already zipping up my skirt and sliding my foot into my glossy, black heels.

"No, I'm good," I said, locating my purse.

But was I? I didn't want to leave his arms, let alone his presence.

Don't look back. Don't look back.

The chant reminded me of the warning given to Orpheus by Hades in Greek Mythology. If I looked back, this magical man would likely vanish, and my night with him would be nothing more than a dream.

Just grab your stuff and leave.

I adjusted the purse strap on my shoulder and placed my hand on the knob. In my mind, I would say, "see ya" and disappear into the night, but when he called out to me, I froze.

"You aren't going to tell me your name?" he said.

Dammit! I couldn't help but look. One last look.

Thank goodness he didn't disappear. As a matter of fact, it was like I was seeing him for the first time all over again, and damn, he was beautiful. His insanely attractive face, flawless chocolate skin, and long sculpted body stretched out on an opulent bed fit for royalty made my knees weak.

Fortunately for me, the headboard carried no traces of the assault it took from a mad woman coming undone. With one arm bent and resting behind his head, Merrick looked completely unbothered and in his element.

I was positive that he was the type of man that could pull me into places I didn't want to go, make me say things that I would later regret, and have me questioning if my choices to avoid commitments were wrong.

Bottom line, he was dangerous. Therefore, I would stick to my original plan.

"My name," I said with exaggerated self-assurance, "is not important. I got what I came for."

Then with great effort, I tore my eyes away and exited the room, already emotionally crushed that I would never get to have sex with him again.

Chapter Two

❖

My best friend's mouth hung open and she held two fingers in the air. I ignored her and took a bite out of my delectable gourmet burger from my absolute favorite burger spot. It had extra pickles and mustard, just the way I liked it.

Mmm Tangy.

Jada and I were in the middle of our bi-monthly girls' night at my place, something we'd stuck to religiously for the past three years.

The evening unfolded just the way it always did: indulging in good food, venting about work and personal drama, and pampering ourselves with a few at-home spa treatments.

By the time we settled in, the familiar routine had worked its magic, leaving me relaxed, lighter, and almost exuberant.

Our time spent decompressing was not only beneficial for my mental health but also for my skin. The yogurt and honey DIY face masks were amazing. After every treatment, my bronze-colored skin was flawless and glowed like the sun.

In addition, I couldn't help but notice the jury seemed far more persuadable when they had something, or rather, someone, pleasant to look at. And honestly, I'd take any advantage I could get.

I placed my burger back on my plate, and Jada ever so

casually pulled the entire tray of food from in front of me and pushed it aside.

"Hey!" I objected through a mouth full of food.

She waved me off.

"Jocelyn, two dicks! Don't you think you've had enough meat for the week?"

I finished chewing and swallowed.

"Not at all," I replied, reaching for my food, but she swatted my hand.

It was my own fault, really. I should have known better than to mention my threesome with two strangers during dinner.

"We are not eating right now. We are talking," Jada said, pushing her food aside as well. "You finally got your fantasy and I want all the details. Who were they? How was it? Awkward? Fantastic? Are you going to see them again?"

I sat back and sighed. At this rate, my stomach was going to eat itself. I hadn't eaten all day, and now I was paying for it, but I knew Jada wouldn't rest until she heard everything.

"Calm down! Their names were Merrick and Xavier." I paused to think about it because now I wasn't sure. "Okay, wait, maybe their names were Morris and Xander. Shit, I don't know."

Jada gaped and gripped the table, stunned.

My poor friend had just closed her mouth after getting over the initial shock, and now here it was, hanging open again.

"You don't even know their names? I know you are no saint, Jocelyn, but that's bold even for you."

"What can I say?" I shrugged. "I was feeling adventurous."

"Clearly. Did *they* at least know each other?"

"Yeah, they were friends. I think since childhood or something, but I was only half listening."

"Too busy trying to get to the sex, huh?" Jada asked.

"You know my motto..."

"Think with your pussy," Jada finished with a laugh. "You act like such a guy sometimes. Sex is always on your mind."

She grabbed a fry and motioned for me to continue. I thought about her questions.

"Let's see," I said, holding up a finger each time I answered. "One was the CEO of a construction company. The other was a professional hockey player who lives in Canada."

"Professional hockey player?!" Jada almost screamed. "Oh, this is too good. Get to the sex. How was it?"

Reaching the almost foot away, where Jada had pushed my tray, I grabbed a fry then dipped it into ketchup. I shoved it into my mouth and took my precious time answering.

I wasn't sure how forthcoming I wanted to be. Not because I didn't want her to know, but because I felt certain I would never have sex that amazing again. The thought kind of dampened my mood.

"It was alright, but mostly because of Merrick/Morris," I said, combining the two names since I was no longer sure.

"Which one is that again?"

"He's the businessman."

"Oh wow, so that means the hockey guy wasn't as talented in bed as he is on the ice?"

I nodded, and Jada seemed a little disappointed.

Guilt washed over me. I hated not being completely truthful with her, but I had no choice.

"Never forget how much you enjoyed being my whore tonight," he had said.

The erotic memories were already forcing their way to the surface.

That's just great, I thought sarcastically. *Now, I'll be spending all night with my vibrator between my legs.*

"I'm sorry, Jocelyn," Jada suddenly said. "You finally get your fantasy and it was only alright."

Yeah, if alright means he had me gasping for air and almost put me in a coma.

"Pretty much," I said. "Don't get me wrong, though. I did have fun."

"So much fun that you don't want to see either of them again," Jada commented snidely, crossing her arms.

She wanted me to meet a guy and fall madly in love, but I wasn't looking for that and she knew it.

Still, Jada hoped that one day I would tire of the sex without commitments lifestyle and things would transform into a romantic love story, but she was wasting her time. I had never had a serious relationship in my life, why break the record now?

"Sorry, girlie," I said, pulling my tray over. "This won't be the romance story you have been waiting for. It was a wonderful night. Now back to my regularly scheduled program."

"Not even with Aaron?" she asked, almost pleading. "He really likes you."

I let out a frustrated grunt. Aaron and I broke up eight months ago, but I kept him around for the sex, even though I hadn't slept with him for over three months.

"Nope. You already know I only keep Aaron around for a good time and because I've known him for years."

"Which is why I don't understand. Obviously, the chemistry is there. What's wrong with giving him a chance?"

"If you like him so much, maybe you should date him?"

Her response was to give me her piercing lawyer stare. I remember we'd both spent hours practicing them on each other, and now they were perfect.

"Jada, Aaron wants something serious and you know I don't do serious relationships. I don't mind the fun dates, but if he is envisioning marriage and kids... I want no part of it."

"You're still going to keep doing that, aren't you?" Jada said, giving me a pitying look.

I knew what she was thinking. The only reason I feared commitment was due to the less-than-favorable marriage my mom had with my stepdad, Gary.

I'll be the first to admit that that definitely didn't help convince me, but it wasn't the reason I avoided commitment.

I simply wasn't interested in it. Besides, I knew healthy relationships existed; I grew up surrounded by one. Before Gary, my parents had been married for twenty years. My dad was the best father and husband my mom and I could have ever asked for.

However, over my adult life, I quickly learned that many men, or at least the ones I attracted, were only interested in one thing... and it wasn't a happily ever after.

They wanted sex and lots of it. Luckily for them, I enjoyed the X-rated sport as much as they did, probably even more so. It was my stress reliever that always delivered and held no empty promises.

If I needed life or mental fulfillment, my career could do that. It allowed me to focus on things bigger than myself, fight for the victims and focus any anger or hurt into something a lot more productive.

"You know," Jada said, cutting into my thoughts. "One day, you will meet a guy that changes all that for you."

"You mean like you have?" I said sarcastically.

Rolling her eyes, Jada pointed a fry at me.

"Listen, smart ass. We both are beautiful, successful, considerate and intelligent women. One day we will find the men that suit us perfectly."

"The yin to our respective yang," I added, poking fun at her.

Jada ignored the tone in my less-than-thrilled response.

"Exactly! Maybe we both are too busy with work and

enjoying life right now, but you mark my words when we least expect it, love will show up."

"You think so?"

"I know so. And when it happens, I will force you into it kicking and screaming if I have to."

Jada's cell began to ring and she excused herself to take the call. I watched her hurry off in her sumptuous white robe, our comfy attire for girl's night, and smiled. We'd been friends for a long time and she was like the sister I never had.

Growing up, I was an only child and although my parents spoiled me with their love and time, I did long for a sibling.

I felt like the odd kid out, always having to invite a friend over for outings at the carnival or theme parks that required me to have a partner. Part of me believed I was at a disadvantage as if something was missing in my life.

Then, when my dad died, I learned firsthand what "missing" truly felt like. His absence subjected me to pain much greater than anything I could have ever imagined.

I had no idea how I would continue to go on, but I eventually did. Unfortunately, I'm not sure I could say the same about my mom.

Staring out of my kitchen window into the night, I felt defeated. My mom had been with Gary, my self-centered asshole of a stepdad, for ten years.

From her perspective, which is quite flawed, Gary pulled her out of a dark tunnel during the lowest point in her life. The truth was if he did pull her out of one miserable reality, it was only because he planned to drown her in another.

My dad was my mom's soulmate and if I thought losing him broke my heart, it completely shattered hers. Days turned into weeks, weeks into months, then, eventually, years, I watched my mother gradually fade away.

At first, the changes were subtle. For instance, she'd cancel our plans at the last minute. When I'd try to reschedule, she'd say she would get back to me but didn't until I pressed her repeatedly.

It didn't take a rocket scientist to see the ever-growing shadows in her eyes or hear the ache that laced her words whenever my father was mentioned. Nevertheless, I believed in time it would get easier.

Well, it didn't.

Two years later, my mom suffered a fall due to dizziness and fatigue. We later learned that she was in the early stages of chronic kidney disease. Everything went downhill fast after that.

She no longer wanted to do anything enjoyable, barely ate, and I was convinced she planned to give up on life altogether and join my dad.

Four years after my father's death, my mom met Gary, and I thought my prayers had been answered.

Suddenly she was getting dressed for dates, laughing easier, and found the courage to pack up my dad's clothes and donate them to a local homeless shelter.

Happiness didn't begin to describe how I felt. I had my mom back, and it seemed our period of suffering had ended. That was until that dreadful day Gary came home drunk.

He'd lost his job and was in a sour mood. My mom tried to be encouraging, but he wasn't hearing it. He was angry at the world and someone had to pay. I guess that unlucky person was my mom because he hit her.

The action was unforgivable to me, but after dozens of apologies, pleadings, and gifts, it appeared my mom didn't share my sentiments.

"Hey, sorry about that," Jada said, approaching the table. Her brows furrowed. "Are you okay? Before I left you seemed happy. Now..." she motioned to my face.

With my mind reeling, my appetite was gone. I got up

from the table and went to the couch, with Jada following close behind.

"I quit my job a few days ago."

Her eyes widened. "At Schneider & Jones? You've worked at that law firm for five years. Why didn't you say anything?"

I gave her a look. She knew better than anyone that I hated sharing my troubles. Jada moved closer to me on the couch and placed an arm around me.

"Now that spontaneous threesome makes a lot more sense," she said more to herself than me. "What happened, Jocelyn?"

"I got a heads up from Vance. You know the guy that keeps me in the loop about all the illegal stuff going on within the company?"

"Yeah."

"Well, all of their underhanded shit is catching up to them. They are about to be sued by a major corporation. From what I gathered, not only is this lawsuit going to bankrupt them, but it will tarnish their name big time. Any lawyer working for them when the suit is filed, involved or not, will be looked at suspiciously as they try to move forward to find new employment. I wasn't sticking around for them to destroy my name too."

"Wow. Is Vance sure?"

I nodded sadly.

"Positive. His brother works for the company that is suing Schneider & Jones. Plus, Vance showed me the paperwork. They are serving the company in less than thirty days."

"Damn. I am so sorry. Any leads on what to do next?"

"I have a few, but nothing that enthuses me. As crooked as they were, I earned an excellent salary. It might be hard to match it."

"That's terrible, Jocelyn. I can't believe you didn't say anything."

"It wouldn't have mattered, but I have to find something fast. On top of my own expenses, I still pay most of my mom's bills."

Jada sat forward abruptly.

"You're still doing that?! I thought Gary would start chipping in when he got that warehouse job."

Even mentioning the name of that atrocious man made my blood boil.

"No, he isn't pitching in. That heartless bastard gambles all his money away. And even though keeping a roof over my mom's head is resulting in sheltering him by default, I don't exactly have a choice."

I sunk back onto the couch and groaned. My frustrations with Gary ran deep, especially since I now suspected he was abusing her. My mom was the sweetest woman in the world and didn't deserve any of this.

Due to her medical issues and age, she couldn't work. However, any money my mom received, she happily offered to me to put towards the bills. I never took it because I could always afford it, but if I didn't find a job soon, that would all change.

"It's going to be alright, Jocelyn. And if you need anything, anything at all, just tell me. I'll be glad to help."

Jada accompanied her encouraging words with a delicate pat on my knee.

I gave her a genuine smile. "Thanks, but I'll be fine. Everything will sort itself out."

"You are always trying to be so strong. It's okay to need help sometimes."

I faced my dear friend and took her hands in mine.

"Jada, your friendship is the best thing you can offer me, and it's all I need. Don't worry. I got this under control."

I did not have this, that, or anything else for that matter, under control. I had officially been unemployed for an entire week and things were not sorting themselves out.

My one possible lead was a legal position at the courthouse. A friend promised to put in a good word for me, and after seeing the giant pay cut I would be taking, I had a few words of my own, but they weren't good.

Needless to say, my usual optimism was taking a rapid nosedive.

All morning, I searched online for other options, but I kept failing to find jobs that collectively met my legal expertise, preferred distance, and salary requirements.

That was until now.

Business lawyer wanted.

Uh-huh, that's me.

At least five years of experience.

Me again.

Located in the heart of downtown Atlanta.

Yes! I only live ten minutes away from the city.

My eyes skimmed faster now, hope building with every word, anticipation tightening in my chest as I searched for the one line that mattered most, *and there it was...salary.*

$55K a year.

I slammed the laptop shut.

At Schneider and Jones, I made $85K a year. My next job would need to meet or exceed that amount.

"Alright," I said aloud. "Get yourself together. You've got this. You have always had this and if anyone can figure it out, you can."

Hearing myself speak calmed the anxiety rising within me. There was no need to worry about anything. Not only had I built up a safety net of almost ten thousand dollars, but I was also resourceful and single. Cutting back on expenses would be easy until I found something suitable.

I quickly did the math. The money in my account could cover me for at least six months. Then, I remembered my mother's expenses, and just like that, I was down to three months.

With another pitiful sigh, I decided to end my suffering early and abandon the job search for today. Tomorrow I would drop off my application at the courthouse and begin my search all over again.

For now, I poured myself a bowl of chips and a tall glass of wine before plopping down on the couch. Briefly, I considered calling Aaron but instantly decided against that.

Our last conversation was three months ago and it did not end well. We'd just had sex, and Aaron must have been lost in the hazy afterglow because he started pressing me to reconsider getting serious with him.

I declined gently at first, trying not to hurt his feelings. I may not have wanted a commitment, but I did want a friend-ship. Aaron was a wonderful guy, attractive, and financially secure. We got along well.

From his perspective, we were the perfect fit. If I could only "let go of my stubbornness," his words, not mine, I would see that I could be happy with him.

The only thing I ended up letting go of was spending time with him after the intended lighthearted conversation turned into a full-fledged argument.

I stormed out and hadn't contacted him since. A few times, he reached out to me, but I didn't answer. We wanted two entirely different things, no need to waste each other's time.

Opening the music app, I pressed play on my jazz playlist

and curled up on the couch for some much-needed mental relaxation.

My time at the courthouse was very productive, which I took to mean my luck was looking up. Not only was I able to drop off my resume, but I also completed an interview with Brandon Sommen, the hiring manager.

Throughout the entire process, Brandon made it abundantly clear that he was very interested in hiring me. I figured he would be since they would be getting a lawyer as qualified as I was for practically pennies.

Then, when he officially offered me the position, I lied and said I would weigh it against my other offers and let him know early next week. I wasn't exactly gung ho about the pay or boring and repetitive cases I would be working on.

Now, with a fail-safe in place and my usual optimistic mood rebuilding itself, I headed towards the courthouse exit.

My phone buzzed inside my purse, and I stopped near a corner wall and checked it. I would hate for it to be a job interview near this part of town and I miss the call.

However, it wasn't a job. It was a lively telemarketer offering me an all-expenses-paid vacation. I politely declined the "deal of a lifetime" and ended the call.

Sliding my phone back into my purse, I felt my stomach tighten and heart kick up a thousand notches when a familiar, panty-wetting, deep male voice said, "Isn't this a pleasant surprise?"

Chapter Three

"I'M NOT INTO WHIPS AND CHAINS."

had to be dreaming.

It was him... the guy from the threesome. And not the cute one with the wonky dick, but the sinfully sexy one that owned my body as no other man had.

He was definitely a lot taller than my five feet five inches, causing me to tilt my head up awkwardly since we were standing so close to one another.

Under the glorious light of day, I had no problem determining that his toned body and extremely attractive features set him apart from most of the men that surrounded us.

I even caught several women stealing admiring glances at him as they walked by.

Up until now, I figured maybe I had imagined his good looks, exquisite charm, and the almost mystical effect he had on my body. But no, he was everything and more.

"Oh, hi umm..."

"Merrick," he interjected, extending his hand. "And please tell me I will have the pleasure of knowing your name this time."

Shaking his hand, I resisted the urge to ask for a quickie by remaining ladylike and giving him my best professional smile.

"It's Jocelyn."

"Nice to officially meet you, Jocelyn."

Come on! I mentally groaned. *This isn't fair. Even the way he says my name makes me want to melt into a puddle all over the floor.*

"What brings you to the courthouse?" Merrick asked. "I hope nothing illegal."

There was no way I was telling him I was unemployed. I'd already slept with the guy, and admitting that I also didn't have a job made me sound pathetic.

"No, I'm being a good girl this time," I said, hoping he caught my flirtatious hint.

I knew the instant he did because his eyes bore into mine so intently I felt like I could see our night of passion replaying through them.

"What about yourself?" I asked.

Lifting a thick white envelope, he said, "I'm dropping off some legal documents for my company. I normally don't take care of this, but we are currently in need of someone to run our legal department."

Alarm bells rang out in my head, but I held my tongue. Working with Merrick would be far too tempting. I'd be trying my hardest to get some boss with benefits action.

We watched each other in silence for the longest time while our eyes communicated what our words could not. I drank in the sight of him like a woman dying of thirst.

Merrick wore navy blue pants with a vest to match and an all-white button-down underneath. His black hair was low and wavy, begging me to reach out and touch it. His brown skin held no blemishes but easily showcased his two deep dimples.

He was perfection.

Nevertheless, all good things must come to an end, and just like the first time, I still hated the idea of leaving him.

"It was nice seeing you again," I said regrettably, "but I must get going."

I assumed my goodbye would be accompanied by my legs carrying me out the door, but they weren't cooperating. It appeared that my body had severed the connection from my brain because it wanted to stay.

Merrick was calling out to it, and I'll be damned if my hardened nipples, aching center, and tingling skin didn't want to hear him out.

"Why don't you let me take you to lunch?" he said.

Nope, I'm good. I thought.

"Sure, why not?" I said out loud instead.

An hour later, we had settled into a booth at a cute little cafe within walking distance of the courthouse. In front of me sat a half-eaten blueberry bagel and a warm cup of honey lavender tea, and laid out before Merrick was an empty plate.

He'd ordered a grilled chicken breast with a side of seasoned vegetables and had since devoured it all.

The man made eating look like a sensual task, and I enjoyed every minute of watching that chiseled jaw work as he chewed and swallowed. I vaguely wondered if his healthy eating was part of the reason his body looked so delectable, then forced myself to pull my mind out of the gutter.

While eating, we engaged in general conversation, warming up to each other.

I was pleased to learn that Merrick was single, with no kids, and had never been married. He reminded me about the construction company he owned with his best friend and business partner, Ashton, but I didn't know that he was also part owner of the hotel where our raunchy rendezvous occurred.

His friend Xavier was back in Canada getting ready for

hockey season and likely only considered our night another wild notch in his belt.

I shared similar information about myself – single, no kids, never married, and over eight years of experience as a business lawyer.

As I took another sip of tea, Merrick's eyes raked over me, spending a noticeable amount of time on my mouth and breasts.

"Being a lawyer suits you," he said. "It fits your personality. Who do you work for?"

I wasn't sure I wanted to answer his question because I didn't want to share too much about myself, but I did so anyway.

"At the moment, no one. But before I quit my job last week, I worked for Schneider and Jones handling the legal matters of their LLC clients."

Merrick lifted his glass of water to his lips. Without taking his eyes off me, he took a sip, then asked, "Why did you quit?"

I grabbed a small piece of my bagel to not only enjoy another doughy, sweet, tart taste of diced blueberries but to buy time.

"They just weren't a good fit for me anymore."

He nodded. I wouldn't be surprised if he could tell I was lying. Undoubtedly those damn observant eyes of his could read me like a book.

"You know this is fate, right?" he said.

"For you, maybe. I don't believe in fate. Life is what you make it."

"Right," he said, stretching out the word. "You're a lawyer and all about logic."

"Yes, I am. What's wrong with that?"

"Nothing at all."

He moved his water aside. I couldn't help but notice his hands. My mind instantly flooded with memories of those hands all over my body... touching me...unraveling me... controlling me.

"Tell me the reason you were at the courthouse?" he asked, disrupting my fantasy.

"I already told you."

"No, you didn't. You dodged the question."

Inwardly I grumbled. I hated when guys asked me questions about my life. It's not like they really wanted to know. Why couldn't we skip the pleasantries and go straight to the sex?

I want your dick, not a date, I thought to myself. Hoping he could read my mind.

Once I told him I didn't have a job, I could predict his next move. He would pretend to care and make a weak attempt at saving the day.

Since he was still waiting on a response, it proved I wasn't telepathic, and I'd need to answer his probing question to get him off my back.

Exhaling, I ran my fingers through my loose, curly hair and gave him a tight smile.

"I was dropping off my resume."

Merrick's brows lifted and his eyes dropped to my mouth again.

"A lawyer with your background and skill set would be an asset at Dual. You should come and work for me."

And there it was, the pretend offer I did not want to hear. I knew it would come up as soon as I divulged my current employment status. Why wouldn't it? He already said at the courthouse that his company needed a lawyer. The natural next step would be to mention it to me.

The problem was, yes, I needed a job, but not a job working for him. The only reason he was even offering it was out of pity. We'd enjoyed a magnificent night together. Now he thought he owed me something. He didn't.

I'd waste my time doing an interview only for him to say the company decided to go another direction. He'd have a clear conscience, and I'd still be jobless. I knew how these things went.

"I don't think working for you would be a good idea," I said, politely.

"Is it because you can't stop thinking about me?" he said.

His arrogance made me laugh and directed the conversation exactly where I wanted it to go, sex.

Hmm, maybe I am telepathic.

"I won't lie, Merrick, you are hard to forget. Any guy that fucks me the way you did, deserves his spot in my top ten."

"Ouch!" he replied, feigning hurt. "And here it was I thought I was your number one."

Oh, he was my number one and we both knew it. Honestly, I was now convinced that what I was having before him wasn't sex, pleasurable rough housing maybe, but definitely not sex.

"You weren't a big deal," I lied. "Plus, you were closer to being number ten than you were to being number one. But who knows, if I ever sleep with you again, maybe you'll have the chance to redeem yourself."

"If you start working for me, my chance can be in a few weeks."

I shook my head and laughed. "Are you always like this? Flirting and saying whatever comes to mind just to get a woman into bed."

"I don't have to lie to get women into bed. They go willingly."

I'll bet they do.

As if I needed proof, our waitress Lacy, came over and cleared the table removing everything except our drinks. The way she stared at Merrick and took extra time wiping the area in front of him wasn't lost on me.

Then she stepped back, smiled, and... *was that a wink?*

"Well," Lacy said, balancing a stack of dishes on her shoulder. "do either of you need anything else? Anything at all?"

Her eyes were on Merrick the entire time, her attraction to him unmistakable.

"I'm fine," Merrick said.

"Me too," I agreed, not that she even looked at me.

"Alright, I will be back shortly with your check," Lacy said.

I kept my thoughts to myself about the waitress. I couldn't fault her for being drawn to Merrick. The woman obviously had good taste. I dove back into the conversation.

"So, if you aren't lying, what exactly are you saying?"

I picked up my tea once again to taste the lovely honey and soothing lavender.

"I'm offering you the job of being," he hesitated a moment, then a smile spread across his face, "my mouthpiece."

I almost spit out my drink.

Covering my mouth, I swallowed and cleared my throat before asking, "What the hell is a mouthpiece?!"

Laughing, Merrick said, "It's slang for lawyer. You've never heard of it?"

"No," I said, already reaching for my phone to do a quick search.

Sure enough, there it was.

The informal/slang definition of "mouthpiece" was a lawyer (or anyone) that speaks on behalf of another person or organization.

"Damn," I said, putting my phone back down. "You learn something new every day. I have never heard of that. Although now that I think about it, I get the correlation. It still sounds kind of dirty, though."

"That's because, in our case, it would be."

I leaned in. He had all my attention. "I like dirty, go on."

"The first night I met you, you gave me one of the best blowjobs I'd had in a long time."

I glanced over my shoulder to make sure no one was nearby. "Okay," I said slowly, trying to follow. "You want me to legally represent your company and suck your dick every day?"

"I want you to legally represent my company, and I will give you the *privilege* of sucking my dick every day... amongst other things."

His assumptive and rude correction should have made me want to flip this table over and storm out of the restaurant, but I won't lie my curiosity was winning out. His unapologetic brashness was somehow sexy to me.

"The privilege? Wouldn't you say that your word choice is not only offensive but a bit possessive?"

"Not at all. I'm a dom and that is how I speak to all of my submissives."

"Ah," I said, understanding dawning. That explained his authoritative vibe and the relentless and ruthless way he took control of me that night. It was unforgettable. Even now, it made me quiver with delight and I wasn't even his sub, which reminded me, "aren't you missing something?"

"Such as," he replied.

"I'm not your submissive, so you have no grounds to talk to me like one," I said.

He whispered his assertive reply. "But you're going to be."

My brows lifted and I pointed to myself.

"Me, Jocelyn Milner, a submissive?" I said it as if repeating it would make him retreat, but of course, it didn't.

Instead, he merely stared at me with those intense, dark brown eyes waiting for my response.

I knew a little about the whole Dominant/submissive thing, albeit mostly from porn, but even then, it did intrigue me. I loved dominant men in the bedroom and preferred them actually, but that didn't mean I was cut out to live that lifestyle.

"I love your enthusiasm, but I don't think so. I'm not into whips and chains."

He laughed, clearly amused by my assumption. Lacy returned and placed a black booklet containing the bill on the table.

I almost reached for it, but Merrick pinned me with a stare. After inserting a $100 bill into it and pushing it toward the edge of the table, he said, "I'm not planning to use any whips on you."

Paying attention to details is second nature to me, so it stood out that he only said whips, not chains.

"And the chains?"

"What will I attach the ropes to if not the chains?" He replied casually.

Dammit!

I had the worst luck. Of course, the first guy to give me the type of sex I have only read about or seen in movies would be into something way out of my league.

"You are serious aren't you?" I whispered. "You want me to volunteer so you can tie me up and beat me for your own twisted sexual hangups?"

"Jocelyn," he said in that commanding tone. "Don't assume that what you have heard about the BDSM community applies to all Doms. Everyone makes their own rules."

"Enlighten me then. What does being your submissive look like?"

"Agree to review the contract and we will discuss everything in full detail."

I studied him. I wanted him now. Screw that contract mess he was offering.

"I am fascinated, Merrick, I'll give you that, but this may

be a bit too much for me. It sounds like I would be agreeing to something complicated when all I really want is the sex."

"Become my submissive and you will have lots of it."

I narrowed my eyes at him and inched closer. My lawyer mode had been activated.

"How many women are you currently sleeping with?"

"Five," he stated without hesitation.

"Shit! All at once?"

"Sometimes," he said with so much insouciance, I was impressed.

"Are they all subs?"

"That's all I deal with."

"And what happens if I sign this agreement? Do I become sub number six?"

"They all go away."

I rolled my eyes in disbelief. There was no way he would do that. We didn't even know each other.

"You expect me to believe you will stop sleeping with all of them to start an arrangement with only me?"

He chuckled. "The lawyer in you shows quite easily. Listen, it's not what you think. For me, this arrangement is a practical decision. The excitement of sleeping with numerous women has died out and become a headache. I'd much rather skip the emotional ties... and the condoms."

Did he say skip the condoms? Oh, this keeps getting more and more indecorous.

"What about STDs or the risk of pregnancy?" I asked.

"As far as STDs, I'm clean. I can provide proof and will require a full medical report on you detailing the same. And as far as the risk of pregnancy, I'm going to go out on a limb and say that you take birth control."

"Aren't you just insightful?" I said sarcastically. "Yes, I'm on birth control, but that doesn't matter. This has danger signs written all over it. What if romantic feelings occur?"

Unbothered, he said, "I am open to a relationship if that's the natural progression. Monogamy doesn't terrify me."

"If you are so open to it, why are you single?"

"Being open to it doesn't mean I easily find what I am looking for."

"In that case, I'll save you some time. Romantically speaking, you aren't looking for me. I don't do relationships."

"That's because you were waiting for me."

Sitting back, I crossed my arms, unsure what to make of this conversation. Lacy appeared and picked up the booklet.

After glancing inside, she said, "I'll be back with your change."

"No need," Merrick replied. "Thank you for everything."

Lacy stared, momentarily in shock. "Seriously! That's over a sixty-dollar tip?"

Merrick smiled politely in response.

"Looks like you're as generous as you are handsome," Lacy complimented. Turning to me she added, "You should definitely keep him."

Lacy better be glad I wasn't a jealous woman, or her head would be involuntarily kissing this floor. That was another reason I didn't do relationships; no worries about cheating. Merrick was free to do what he wanted.

When she was out of earshot, I said, "I don't know if I want to keep you. You seem like a lot of trouble."

"Only the good kind, I promise. Will you agree to my offer?"

"I'm thinking about it. Let's discuss the legal position." I said and began to fire off questions.

"How do you know I would be a good lawyer for your company?"

"Call it a hunch."

"What if your hunch is wrong?"

"I'll fire you without hesitation."

"Don't you have to run it by your business partner first?"

"He trusts my judgment."

"And what if I get angry and sue you for sexual harassment?"

"Again, there's a contract, remember?"

I shook my head. He had an answer for everything.

"How much does this position pay?"

"I haven't decided." He drummed the table with his fingers and seemed to consider it. "What was your salary at your previous employer?"

"Eighty-five thousand," I said, confident he wouldn't match it.

"How does doubling that sound?"

My eyes bulged.

"You're going to pay me that much to have sex with you?"

"No, I will pay you that much to run our legal department, and trust me, you will earn every cent. The workload is extremely heavy and it takes up a lot of time. As far as being my submissive, I'm not going to pay you anything for that. You will do it because you want to."

I rolled my eyes.

"Sounds like I'm signing up to give you free ass."

He released a low, deep chuckle, "And yet, I've already fucked you for free, remember?"

I bit my lower lip, my enjoyment of that memory evident in my response. "Oh, I do remember."

"The point is, beautiful, I don't think there is a price high enough to offer you in exchange for the pleasure of doing it consistently."

"So you went with free?" I exclaimed. "I mean, I'm no prude, so if you offered me an additional twenty thousand for sex, I wouldn't be offended."

"Alright, done," he said.

I laughed, but he didn't.

Oh shit, he isn't joking!

I exhaled and sat back in my chair. "I was kidding, Merrick."

"I wasn't. I believe you are what we need at Dual, and I know for a fact you would be a perfect sub."

I studied him. Undoubtedly he had money. Curious as to how high he would go, I tossed out another number.

"Thirty thousand."

Merrick sat back and remained silent so long I didn't think he would respond. When he did, it was once again something I didn't expect.

"Give me your hand."

It was an odd request, but I reached across the table and deposited my hand into his. The connection between us sparked to life immediately. His hands were big, warm and soft, just like I remembered the night he used them to hold me in place and bang the breath out of me.

I had to stop this shit. What was it about him that pulled me in and made me want more?

Merrick moved his thumb ever so gently over the top of my hand. I sucked in a breath, anticipating his next words. My pussy was on fire.

Damn his gorgeous face and charismatic ways!

"Jocelyn, we both know this isn't about money but control. Therefore, I am not going to insult you by having a tactless negotiation over your body. In my mind, you are priceless."

I just stared at him like a damn idiot.

He kissed my hand, placed it on the table and stood. Before exiting the restaurant, he looked down at me and said, "I expect to hear from you by 9 o'clock tonight, agreeing to give me what I want."

Chapter Four

"WHAT'S YOUR SAFE WORD?"

I traveled down a long dark road with nothing in sight. Not one house, gas station, or other vehicle had been spotted for several miles as I drove further and further into the night toward an unknown destination.

I was certain that I was lost, but Merrick, speaking to me through my Bluetooth, assured me that I wasn't.

Who lived out in the middle of nowhere?

Giving up wasn't something I did often, but in this case, I might have to throw in the towel. As bad as I wanted to see Merrick and enjoy another night of passion, I now felt out of place.

Being alone and proceeding down this winding dark road had me rethinking everything – accepting the job at Dual and being his fuck toy, or whatever he called it. Maybe it was all too much. Spontaneity could be fun, but this was wildly impetuous.

The words, "Let's do this another time," were on their way out of my mouth when the road suddenly opened up, and a huge building stretched out before me.

In awe, I slowed to stare at it. It looked like a medieval castle. This could not be where Merrick lived. Count Dracula, maybe, but not a lively, handsome, single, CEO.

I glanced at the clock. It was 10:30 pm. When we spoke on

the phone at 9, per his request, he asked me to be here by ten, and although I hated being late, I liked pushing his buttons more.

"I see you," Merrick said. "Unlock your door, but do not get out of the car."

He ended the call and I began turning in all directions to check my surroundings.

Why did he say not to get out of the car? Was this a dangerous area or something?

I knew thinking with my pussy was going to get me into trouble one day, which was totally unfair.

Men thought with their dicks all the time, and they survived... *well, that one guy didn't,* I thought. concerning a gruesome murder I'd heard about. *Boy, did she do a number on him.*

The point was, I might end up dead all because I couldn't resist a booty call.

I watched Merrick approach. He was all confidence and sex appeal wrapped into one. He opened my car door and extended his hand, helping me out.

"Is everything okay? Why didn't you want me to get out of the car?"

"Everything is fine, gorgeous. I simply wanted to open the door for you."

Good looking and a gentleman. I could get used to being around him.

"Why are you late?" he asked.

Up close, the building looked even more massive and intimidating. My eyes traveled the length of it before the structure disappeared behind a clutter of giant trees.

There were probably close to thirty cars in the parking lot, but they were very spread out.

"I guess I drive slow," I lied.

"Next time, leave earlier. I don't tolerate tardiness."

"Is that one of the rules for your submissives?"

"It is," Merrick said.

"Do you have others?"

"I do, but you will learn-as-you-go."

He was still holding my hand. He hadn't let it go since he helped me out of the car. Although simple, I found the gesture intimate and it made me feel safe.

I glanced up at him as we continued our slow pace toward the door. In response, he gave me a look that made my lower half, way too excited.

"What happens if I don't follow them?" I asked.

"I suggest you don't fuck around and find out," he said with a grin, his dimples making him appear innocent and jovial.

I knew he was being serious but his tone was always so easygoing it put me at ease. I couldn't wait to have him, or rather he, have me, on the regular, but for now, I was going to play this cool.

"I expect that you have a lot of questions for me. I always want you to feel free to ask anything and everything you wish to know. My goal is to make you feel as comfortable as possible," he said.

That was a relief because this whole Dominant/submissive arrangement was fascinating. Endless questions swam around in my head, but I assumed I wasn't supposed to ask until he presented me with the contract.

"What is this place? I was expecting to go to your house."

"I don't take subs to my house. That is something you have to earn, and this place is called Iron Kink. It's an elite, private BDSM club that gives clients a fun, safe place to play, meet, and mingle."

The idea that this world had rules, boundaries, and a certain level of sophistication both intimidated and impressed me.

"Is this where I should meet you from now on?" I asked.

"No, this may be the first and last time I bring you here. However, I think it sets a good tone for what I expect from you."

"Okay," I said slowly, "So if we won't be meeting here for sex or at your place, how do I get laid?"

Just hearing his infectious laugh made driving down that long winding road, fearing I was about to be a victim in a horror film, worth it.

"I love your sense of humor," he said. "And in answer to your question, don't worry I am very creative."

My attention went back to the building. As sexually uninhibited as I was, I had never been to a sex club.

We made our way to a tall, sleek black door with a gold doorbell shaped like a face and a blindfold covering the eyes.

Merrick pressed the button and immediately I heard a voice over the intercom say, "Name?"

"Sir Alexander," Merrick said.

There was a buzzing noise, then Merrick pulled the huge door open.

"After you," he said.

I stepped inside and looked around, spotting nothing and no one – just a long, dimly lit hallway with walls the color of red velvet and paintings of people in various sex positions.

"From this point on, you are to address me as sir."

I half giggled and playfully rolled my eyes. My attention was on an image of a woman chained to a bed and eight naked men standing over her.

The sarcasm seeped through my words when I said, "Okay, sir, whatever you say."

Merrick spun me around and had my back against the wall in seconds, his hands on either side of my head, boxing me in.

My heart sped up, and my chest heaved, surrounded by his

scent and power, as ambiguous emotions awakened within me.

I'd never met anyone like him before. I wanted things with him, from him, for him, and I didn't understand why.

Merrick leaned in so that his mouth was close to my ear. "You see Jocelyn, what you're doing is fucking around. Now, before you find out what I'm capable of, I strongly suggest you show me some respect."

Did it just get warm in here? What was happening to me?

What my mind couldn't comprehend, my body could. Merrick was pure dangerous temptation and I wanted in on it. He backed away only mere inches to stare into my eyes.

"Consider that rule number two."

This time, there was no teasing in my tone when I said, "Yes, sir."

Pushing away from the wall, Merrick took my hand, and we began walking again. From the pace we were moving, I assumed he was giving me a tour, wanting me to take it all in and determine if I could handle it.

"I can only imagine the type of sexual depravity that goes on behind these walls," I said, my eyes darting around, noticing several plain black doors.

"You're looking at it from a judgmental perspective. What you call depravity, others call preference. I'm sure you of all people, can understand that it's okay to be into different things. Besides, nothing happens here without consent."

I considered his response and instantly felt guilty. He was right. I was the pot, judging the kettle.

"You do have a point. I certainly can't judge people for what they're into. Especially since I use sex like a pain pill."

"Elaborate?"

"Sex is like a drug for me. It calms, or in some cases numbs, my emotions and gets me out of my head. Afterward, I feel balanced and focused."

"I understand."

His response was so simple, yet somehow I felt like a giant weight had been lifted. I had never confessed that to anyone before.

"So this is really a whole lifestyle for you?" I asked, still a bit astonished.

"It is."

At the end of the hall, we turned right and headed towards a large, winding staircase. Several closed doors had the words "Aftercare" engraved on them.

"What's aftercare?" I asked.

"It's where the Dom takes their sub after a session. It allows for the involved parties to support one another, tend to wounds, or generally check in."

Tend to wounds? Were we still talking about sex?

I wasn't going to tackle what he meant by wounds head-on, so I came from it another way.

"And you've done tons of wild stuff to your subs before, like bondage? And spankings?"

Merrick made a sound similar to a low laugh. Then he glanced at me and said, "Oh, Jocelyn, that's on the light side. Don't forget collaring, humiliation, caging and breath play. Those are some of my favorites."

"Caging?" I tried to say it cooly, but it came out in a squeak. It wasn't helping that the word "Wounds" still flashed repeatedly in my mind like a warning sign.

"It's when the sub is confined within a cage, giving the Dom the feel of ownership and control over them."

I swallowed hard. If he weren't still holding my hand I might try to bolt. This was a lot.

"How do you know that you won't seriously injure them or go too far?"

"It's my job to know what's too far. Anything I do in my

role as a Dom is not to be taken lightly and I do not abuse my power."

My mind was blown. This was some hardcore shit. He had done things I'd never even heard of and while some sounded interesting, others were deeply terrifying.

"But...you aren't trying to do all those things to me, are you?"

"No."

I waited for him to say more, but he didn't, which meant I would have to ask yet another question. I was starting to believe this was part of his technique to pull me out of my comfort zone.

"No, to which ones?" I asked.

Merrick stopped and faced me, my hand still settled, albeit shakily, in his.

"Hey, look at me," he said, directing my eyes to his. They were full of compassion and patience. "I promise you, everything I do to you, you will want done. I am not going to harm you and I am not a sadist."

That made me feel better. However, he'd just mentioned another term I wasn't fully familiar with. I should ask him if he can give me a book on terms to study.

I grasped a much better understanding when I read things. Hours spent in the library with my head buried in a book helped me pass all of my law classes with flying colors. Maybe a book is what I needed here.

"I apologize for asking so many questions, and I hate to sound so naive, but define sadist?"

"Never apologize for needing clarification or having questions. I already told you I want you to feel as comfortable as possible. This is all new to you and it can be overwhelming." He faced away and we started walking again. "A sadist is a person who enjoys seeing or gets off on inflicting pain on others. And before you ask, yes people consent to that because for them, being subjected to that pain is how they receive their sexual gratification. They are called masochists."

Now that he'd explained, I recalled hearing the meaning before but always mixed the two up. Something tells me I wouldn't be forgetting the meaning of either word ever again.

I was feeling better, my shoulders were relaxed and I was breathing easier.

Everything is fine.

Or I thought it was until I heard a woman scream. I almost jumped out of my skin and yanked my hand from Merrick's hold, not needing to see the panic in my expression to know it was there.

My eyes found his, and I began to back away, but before I put too much distance between us, Merrick's arm shot out and stopped me, pulling me close.

"It's okay, Jocelyn."

"But someone's screaming," I said. "What's going –"

"Yes, more! More!"

Now, sheer enjoyment laced the woman's high-pitched screams.

Merrick stared down at me.

"She's simply enjoying her spanking session with Blaze, that's all. Let's go."

"Blaze?" I said, not moving an inch.

Merrick placed a hand on my shoulder and ushered me forward.

"He's another Dom and a good friend of mine. You'll meet him, eventually."

The hell I would! I didn't want to meet anyone that would have me screaming for dear life.

We descended the stairs, and he led me to a room with a door that read "Sir Alexander".

After unlocking it, he held it open and waited for me to

enter. Once I was safely inside, with nowhere to run, Merrick closed the door and leaned against it.

He remained silent, watching me while I took it all in. The room was a pleasant surprise – small, clean and not terrifying at all. Soft grey walls gave the room a cozy feel, and it smelled of fresh rosemary and geranium.

I turned to my right and found a wall decorated with more steamy photos like those in the building's hallway entrance, provoking salacious urges that I hoped Merrick would fulfill soon.

As I continued to slowly spin, I was faced with a large wall that held several hooks placed high and low.

I don't want to imagine what those are for.

The next area contained a large bed, a giant mirror, a chair attached to a metal pole behind it, and, in the corner, the biggest box I had ever seen.

I was a few inches over five feet tall and that box must have almost reached my shoulder. I was positive it contained instruments of torture, or fun, depending on how you looked at it.

A second look at the chair revealed bondage straps on the arms and legs.

I hope I don't end up in that tonight.

The beam behind the chair stretched all the way up the extremely high ceiling. It must have been over ten feet tall, and I wondered why that was but wasn't going to ask.

Now, I was back facing Merrick. He was still leaning against the door, but his hands were behind his back. This was the first time tonight I truly took in the sight of him. Now that I had, the reason why I was here became crystal clear.

I wanted Merrick anyway, and anyhow, I could get him. If I had to become his submissive in order to do that, then I was willing.

Dressed in navy blue jeans and a black, collared shirt... his expression captured me. To put it plainly, Merrick looked like a sexy bad boy, up to no good, and because I couldn't resist temptation, I wanted in on all the trouble.

"So what now?" I asked. My voice was low and soft.

"Take off your clothes."

With instant obedience, I pulled my shirt over my head and slid my jeans over my hips.

After removing everything, I placed my hands at my sides and awaited his instructions.

"In the box on the bed, I have something for you. Go put it on."

I moved towards the bed, the soft wool carpet, a pleasant feeling underneath my bare feet. Opening the box, I found two items; A red, full-body leather harness covered in tiny diamonds and a masquerade-looking mask to match. They were stunning.

The harness was laid out in a way that resembled a leotard, but where a leotard actually covered the body this one explicitly revealed it.

Lifting it from the package, I held it up and turned to Merrick.

"Do you like it?" he asked.

"Yes sir, it's beautiful," I replied, pulling it on.

After fastening the last buckle, I spent a few minutes modeling it around the room for him.

With the exception of the straps that connected between my thighs, ran up my sides, under my breasts, and fastened around my neck, I was completely nude. Regardless, I felt elegant and totally comfortable.

Merrick hovered close, admiring my body, the thick bulge in his pants revealing just how much he liked it. However, I noticed he didn't touch me.

"Your breasts and ass look spectacular in this," he complimented.

I smiled with appreciation.

"Before we begin," he continued. "I need you to do something for me."

"Anything, sir," I replied.

"Even though there should be no cause for it since tonight is only a tester for you, I would still like for you to give me a safe word. If you are uncomfortable, in pain, or simply want out of the scene, you say that word, and I will end it."

Immediately my mind conjured a word, or rather a phrase, that I knew would snap me out of the moment, end the fantasy and remind me that life and people could be cruel.

It was something I used to love, but due to an ugly and hurtful memory, I could no longer stomach the sight of them. "Red rose," I said confidently.

Chapter Five

Merrick's brows lifted. "Red rose," he repeated.

I silently prayed he didn't ask me why I wanted to use those words and was overcome with relief when he didn't.

"Red rose it is," he said, stepping aside. "Go sit in the chair."

I sat down, scared, excited, and obviously out of my fucking mind to allow a man I barely knew to strap me down.

"What I am doing is a simple chair bondage technique," Merrick said. "I am going to tie your ankles to the legs of the chair and your arms to the tops of each armrest."

I kept quiet, only moving when he instructed me to test the first restraint on my left ankle. It was nice and tight but didn't hurt.

Currently, my only discomfort was my pussy. It was throbbing so hard that I was surprised Merrick couldn't physically see it.

"Will you always tie me up when we have sex?"

Merrick finished the leg straps and started on my arms.

"Most of the time, yes."

"Why?"

"Because agreeing to be my sub means you surrender your power to me. Tying you up helps me keep that power."

49

"What about the times you don't tie me up?"

"You are to refrain from moving and not touch me."

"Wait! I can't touch you, ever?"

"Not unless I instruct you to. Like everything else, you have to earn it. But don't look so sad, beautiful, not allowing you to touch me makes things more intense for you."

"How so?" I asked, bewildered. I couldn't believe this! Denial of touching that magnificent body of his was punishment all in itself.

Merrick studied me, leaned down really close and bit his lower lip. He was so hot when he did that.

I could smell the fresh mint on his breath, see the thick lashes that outlined his seductive eyes, and feel the power radiating from his body.

"Let me paint you a picture," he said. His mouth inches from mine. "Has a guy ever eaten your pussy so good that once you came, you were too sensitive for him to keep going?"

I nodded. The question alone made me wetter.

"Well, with me, you won't get out of it that easy. I want to find out what happens when you're pushed past your limits, and if you're free to touch me, you might try to stop me."

He traced a finger over my slightly parted lips and slid it into my mouth. Closing my eyes, I sucked on it, envisioning it was his dick.

Only moments later, Merrick pulled his finger free and I released a whimper. I wanted a taste of him no matter how I had to get it.

Following his movements, I watched him reach for a silver electrical box. It was attached to the wall next to the chair and displayed two black buttons.

"What's that?" I asked.

"A control panel. It lifts the chair."

"That's interesting. Why does it need to lift?"

"Because being on your knees is your job, not mine," he said and pushed the button.

The chair raised quicker than I thought possible. It was smooth and quiet, only releasing a small mechanical purr as it brought me face-to-face with Merrick.

He released the button and gathered my hair in his hands. After sliding it to one side to reveal my neck, Merrick proceeded to kiss and lightly nip my earlobe and neck. Tilting my head further to allow him easier access, I sighed.

Between slow sensual kisses, he said, "Please feel free to ask me more questions. Later you won't be able to."

I swallowed, taking in the feel of his soft lips working their way down my body. He was now at my collarbone, his fingers delicately caressing my waist.

I balled up my fist.

I can handle this. I don't need to touch him. I can hold my composure just fine.

"Umm..." I said, trying to form the words to ask a question that seemed so important before his mouth was brushing up against my skin. "If I agree to be your sub, what type of things can I expect to be subjected to?"

"Bondage, of course," he answered, kissing the swell of my left breast. "I will restrain you so that all the control belongs to me and the only pleasure you receive is what I am willing to give."

"Yes, sir," I said in a voice no louder than a whisper.

"Exhibitionism," he said next, sucking my nipple into his mouth, then grazing the tip with his teeth, causing me to cry out. "I expect you to take pleasure in being watched and used by me in public."

"I understand, sir," I moaned.

Was it merely my imagination because I was pulling against them or were these restraints getting tighter?

"Degradation," Merrick added. Giving my right breast the

same treatment as the left. "You will happily accept and show gratitude for being treated like the slut that you are."

"I will, sir," I said, moving my hips, which was pointless because with my ankles bound, I couldn't move much.

I was so lost in the titillating world of pleasure I didn't even hear the chair rise higher, but I felt Merrick's tongue travel downward, kissing my stomach and navel area, drawing closer to my pussy.

I opened my eyes and watched his head dip lower and lower, his black, wavy hair begging to be touched.

Merrick licked his lips and said, "Punishment," before gliding his long tongue all over my pussy. "You will learn to have respect, and if you get out of line, I might deny you orgasms or force you to have so many that you pass out."

That's it! I was lying to myself. I couldn't hold my composure. I wanted free of these restraints.

I opened my mouth to respond, but words didn't make it. Only sounds did. Merrick's tongue was lethally talented and I was experiencing sheer bliss under his touch.

After a few minutes of toying with me until I felt like screaming, Merrick dragged his tongue up my slit and then paused. With his mouth merely inches away from my clit he whispered, "And rewards." Then he closed his lips around my swollen bud and sucked hard.

I. Lost. My. Shit.

Some wild version of myself yanked at the restraints, whimpered, begged and pleaded. Basically, if it came to mind, I did it. I wanted desperately to close my thighs and pause this debilitating tongue attack Merrick was performing on me.

Spreading me wider so that my clit was fully exposed, he gave me no mercy. Sucking, pulling, and lapping at my center until I shouted. My head fell back, colliding with the cushioned back of the chair and I squeezed my eyes shut.

I wanted more... I wanted less... I wanted out of this damn chair.

"I'm about to cum," I cried out, almost over the edge, then suddenly it was over because he stopped. Just fucking stopped!

"No, you aren't," he said. "Because that brings us to rule number three. You do not cum without my permission."

My eyes popped open and I glared at him.

"You're... kidding," I said, pulling in air like I hadn't drawn in a sufficient amount since he began touching me.

"I assure you, I'm not."

"This sucks ass," I said under my breath.

Merrick laughed and waved a finger. "No, no, no. Gratitude, remember?"

I drew in a deep breath, then slowly released it.

Don't be late... refer to him as sir... don't cum without permission.

All of these rules had me aggravated.

"Thank you, sir, for *almost* making me cum," I said through clenched teeth.

I couldn't help my annoyance. I had been so close.

"If you were my sub, that condescending tone would earn you a punishment, but since you have yet to sign the contract, you're safe... for now."

He lowered the chair, untied me and helped me stand. I kept my mouth shut because if I said anything it wouldn't be nice.

Merrick grabbed the mask from the bed, then pulled a thick leather restraint with two holes in it from the giant box in the corner.

"Put your arms behind your back," he instructs.

I do so with an irritated huff, and he bounded them with the leather restraint before turning me to face him.

"Close your eyes and stop pouting before I decide to punish you after all."

Carefully, I felt him place the mask over my eyes and tie it behind my head. Tilting my chin upward, he turns my face from side to side. I wait, my eyes still closed, assuming he is checking the mask, but out of nowhere, Merrick's lips cover my own.

I sigh and stand on tiptoes, tasting the sweet, salty flavor of my pussy on his tongue. As his mouth takes possession of mine, I am blown away by how much I need this.

Reaching down, Merrick rubs his hands over my exposed breasts, squeezing my nipples. All too soon he ends the kiss and I am left with my entire body on fire.

He's smiling at me when I open my eyes, checking me out from head to toe.

"How do I look?" I ask.

"Like a mysterious slut," he replies, "which is exactly what I wanted."

I glanced over at the full-length mirror. Merrick was right. The straps I was wearing left nothing to the imagination, and the mask was akin to something you would wear at a luxurious ballroom party.

"Are you ready to become my sub yet? If you are, we can skip this next part."

I was ready, so ready, but I was curious as to what he had planned next.

"No, I'm still considering your offer," I announced.

"Alright then." Grabbing my arm, he pulls me toward the door. "Let's go"

I take several steps forward, then stop.

One would think my hesitation came from me being practically nude and not knowing where Merrick was taking me, but it wasn't.

At the moment, I was running on pure adrenaline and convinced I could take on anything. *Well, anything except...*

"You aren't taking me to that screaming room, are you?" I asked cautiously.

"No, lovely. Instead, I have a great show planned for you."

He guided me through numerous twists and turns then down another long hallway. This place was like a maze, and with how far we were going, I was thankful it wasn't cold inside this building, or else I would suffer from frostbite.

Along the way, we passed a few people that slowed to admire my body. Each time, Merrick would have me stop and stand still so that they could get a good look.

Being on display felt so erotic.

Once they moved on, Merrick said, "No one is allowed to touch you, but if people want to look at you, then it should be welcomed don't you agree?"

"Yes sir, I do," I replied.

"You're a fast learner."

We eventually arrived at our destination; a spacious, well-decorated room filled with women either dressed similarly to me or wearing nothing at all.

"This is one of the club's sub-areas," Merrick said.

I smiled, feeling incredibly freaky. Now, this was more my style.

All around me, people were engaged in some sort of sexual activity. To the far left, a group of women were bound and bent over chairs as several men took turns pounding into them.

Next to that were women in cages. Their heads stuck out through the bars, and they couldn't move as people stopped by and stuck fingers, dicks and even dildo-looking objects into their holes.

To the far right, which also happened to be the direction Merrick was pulling me, must have been blowjob central because women were on their knees servicing lines of men.

I even saw a woman being face fucked so hard that she

turned bright red. Next to them, I spotted a guy cum into a shot glass and give it to his sub to drink.

Okay, maybe all of this isn't necessarily my style. This room put my porn collection to shame.

We stopped multiple times for Merrick to greet people and to avoid running into naked women being led around the room on leashes; good thing the carpets were soft.

I saw someone that I thought I knew and off instinct looked away. Mentally I thanked Merrick for giving me a mask to wear. I would hate for someone I knew to recognize me.

"Everyone in this area is regularly checked for STDs and operates with privacy, discretion and respect. You will notice that some subs are taken while others," he nodded to a line of naked women standing against the wall, "are waiting to be of service."

We stopped ten feet in front of a luxurious teal couch and Merrick's hold tightened on my shoulder.

"It is time for the final stage in our night. Your instructions are simple. Don't think, don't speak just get on your knees and observe."

He lowered me to the floor, before going to the couch and facing me again. What he did next, I wasn't prepared for on any level.

He stripped. I'm talking completely naked, leaving not a stitch of clothing on. At this point, the few straps I was wearing meant I was more covered than he was.

Hello, fantasy.

Merrick's body was a work of art; long, lean muscles covered by smooth brown skin and hard abs that led to a long, thick dick.

After taking a seat, he stretched his arms across the back of the couch and snapped his fingers.

One of the subs standing against the wall stepped forward and came over to get down on her knees in front of Merrick.

I couldn't believe what was happening. *Was he really about to make me watch this?*

I squared my shoulders as best as I could with my hands restrained and looked directly at him, forcing myself not to give him a reaction.

Since the sub's back was to me, I wouldn't have been able to see her performance. However, Merrick took care of that because he instructed her to shift to the side of him.

The new positioning reminded me of the time I gave Aaron head in the car. The risk of being caught gave me such a rush, but that was nothing compared to the adrenaline and desire coursing through my veins right now.

Merrick looked me dead in the eyes and said to the sub, "You may begin."

And without even the slightest reservation, sub girl started sucking his dick. Her head bobbed up and down with a steady, sensual rhythm that I had to admit was sexy as hell.

Her loose hair fell over the side of her face, obstructing my view, but Merrick reached down and pulled it back, ensuring I got an eye full.

I was livid, annoyed, irritated, excited, mesmerized and baffled. I hated seeing her please him. It should have been me taking care of his needs, yet, I couldn't look away. The woman moaned, slurped and sucked with such vigor as she worked him in and out of her mouth.

Watching her intently, I got so lost in her enthusiasm and enjoyment I felt like I could taste him in my mouth too.

She used no hands and took him all the way down her throat like a pro, which, given his size, was no easy task.

My eyes lifted back up to Merrick's. He was still watching me, as I sat on the edge, burning with need. I pulled my feet together and sat back, the heel of my foot pressing into my pussy doing a poor job of relieving the pressure I felt, but something was better than nothing.

Sub girl moved upward and spent several moments focusing on the tip of his length before dipping her head low again.

Merrick closed his eyes and leaned his head back.

Damn, I could relate.

If she kept going, he was going to cum and so was I. This was all so wrong, but so erotic that I found myself not wanting her to stop.

She looked so good servicing him that I wanted him to explode in her mouth, forcing her to swallow every drop of his warm release before pushing her aside like the nasty sluts we both were and then coming over to fuck me in front of everyone.

However, I got something much better. Merrick pushed her head down, holding her in place for so long that it made me moan. Then he used her hair to pull upward, freeing himself from her mouth.

He stood and walked over to me, stopping when his dick was mere inches from my face.

"Now, should I let her finish me off? Or, are you ready to be my whore and get on with your job?"

I stared up past his hard dick to his captivating face. I could say it was the "anything goes" vibe around this place or even the fact that Merrick had already started my engine earlier and I was ready to cross the finish line, but the truth was it wasn't either of those.

It was him. Something about him.

His presence sparked a sudden snap of obedience that roused an inner longing to satisfy him. His pleasure was tied to my own and I got off by getting him off.

"I'm ready to be your whore, sir."

Merrick stepped closer and I opened my mouth, not giving a damn that less than a moment before he was getting sucked off by another woman.

His dick, his moans and his release belonged to me.

Holding my head still, he pumped his manhood in and out of my mouth. A small group of people gathered to watch and I remembered that this was what he wanted.

For me to learn to enjoy being of service to him while others watched.

Well, he could cross that off the list because I was hooked.

Abruptly, he told me to get up on my knees, and I did, while he stroked himself to completion, coating my face with his release.

This was officially my first facial and while it was messy, the pleased look on his face made it all worth it. Cum dripped from my chin and landed on my thigh, but I didn't dare take my eyes off him.

"You get to swallow your treat once you sign the contract. Until then, get used to this position while I go over there and have a drink."

And that is how he left me for the rest of the night. On my knees, bound, wet, exposed and covered in his cum.

I had never been so turned on in my life.

Chapter Six

"I LIKE THAT YOU'RE A SCREAMER."

I wrote my signature for what had to have been the 30th time that morning. I was starting to hate my name.

Jocelyn Milner, Jocelyn Milner, Jocelyn Milner, over and over again.

Each document required for the lawyer position, such as W-2s, health insurance, oaths, etc. had been signed and sealed in a vanilla envelope.

I was now signing the Dom/sub sexual contract and Merrick had ensured his ass was covered in this agreement.

Reading through the paperwork made things quite clear. Although the roles of lawyer and submissive were separate positions, the punishment for my breach of contract could (and likely would) terminate both.

For example, if I slept with someone other than Merrick, which only breaks a rule within my submissive contract, it could result in immediate termination and/or a fine of up to $100,000.

Placing Dual in any situation that causes damages or loss to the company could result in the same.

Talk about steep.

Since the law was what I lived for, I took contracts extremely serious which made my signing this all the more insane.

What if I couldn't keep up with his demands? What if I didn't want to?

I flipped back to the first section of the contract and scanned it again.

I, Jocelyn Milner, of sound mind and body (I was signing this contract so my sanity was questionable) *agree to the submission of my sexual will to Merrick Alexander.*

As my Dominant, Merrick will take me into his care and guidance and encourage our growth together in trust and mutual respect.

As his submissive, I will take pleasure and pride in granting him unrestricted use of my body for the fulfillment and enhancement of both of our sexual needs...

The contract went on and on for several more pages with the same subservient tone, but the first part pretty much summed it up. From a sexual standpoint, I was to be his and only his.

I glanced up at Merrick, watching me with a smoldering gaze. He was every fantasy I ever had all wrapped up in one and I wanted him to do every nasty thing to me he craved.

We had already verbally established rules, limits, punishments, boundaries, etc. All that was left for me to do was finish signing my part then he could sign his. I repositioned my pen over the dotted line.

"I plan on taking you out to dinner at the end of your first official week to celebrate you joining the team," Merrick suddenly stated.

"You know," I said, pausing again, "after signing all of these documents, I am not sure my fingers will be able to hold a fork."

Merrick laughed.

"What can I say? I have to protect myself. You could fall madly in love with me and want to sue."

I scoffed, "You wish."

"Maybe, I do," he said.

I cut my eyes at him. "I am signing up for the dick, Merrick. Give the romance to someone else."

"You're so ruthless," he said. Then, in a mischievous tone, he added, "The things I am going to do to you."

"I certainly hope so," I said suggestively.

Flipping to the next page, I took some time to read the fine print. Two pointers stood out to me: No condoms, and without good reason, I was never allowed to deny him sex or access to my body.

Below it was a list of my non-negotiable rules; no abuse, blood play, or anal play to name a few.

To Merrick's credit, this contract was straightforward and fair. There were no vague conditions or hidden clauses. The only thing I had to battle with was my nerves and morals. I never thought I would be doing something like this.

In actuality, I think I could deal with most things on a personal level, but I didn't want this contract to interfere with me professionally. That was a foundational rule that both Merrick and I had. This arrangement was not to hinder or demolish our respective business reputations in any way.

"Everything okay?" Merrick asked, studying me.

"It's fine." I put the pen down for a second to flex my fingers. "Is your business partner fine with this? Or does he not even know that you are combining personal and business roles with the company."

"He knows. He actually has a mouthpiece of his own."

I laughed again and shook my head.

"So you both are running around town, claiming women and getting two-for-one deals?"

"Pretty much," he said casually.

"Who's idea was the whole mouthpiece position, anyway?"

"Ashton came up with the idea. I came up with the name."

"Does his lady of choice work here?" I asked, scribbling my name on another document.

I only had five left to review and sign.

"She does. Her name is Shelia, and she is the receptionist for Dual's international client department. I am sure you will meet her eventually."

I was amazed that he was openly sharing such privileged information about his business partner. However, when I arrived at the next page, I understood why. It was another non-disclosure agreement, this particular one, concerning anything I knew about his business partner.

"How long do you anticipate this contract will last between us?"

"Not sure. Why do you ask?"

With indifference, I said, "Because I assume I'll tire of you rather quickly and be ready to move on to another guy."

Merrick smirked and leaned forward. "When I'm done with you, Jocelyn, you won't have anything left to give another man."

That sounded like a tantalizing threat I wanted to see manifested.

Not giving me the chance to respond, Merrick got up from his chair and adjusted his tie. My eyes were elated by the large dose of eye candy they were receiving.

"It looks like you are almost done signing everything and I have a meeting to attend. When you are done, place those documents in the black envelope and bring them to my office. The vanilla envelope needs to go to HR. You can drop that off with Amber at the front desk and she will also direct you to my office."

"Yes, sir," I said.

Something naughty flashed in his eyes, and in my gut, I knew I would soon find out what it meant.

"Hi, how may I help you?"

"Hi, you're Amber, right?" I asked, waiting for her confirmation before giving her my quick spiel and new hire paperwork. The name tag on the desk only read "Receptionist".

She gave me a big friendly smile. "Yes, that's me."

Amber was a cute girl. She was well dressed, likely in her early twenties and appeared to have a very vibrant personality.

"Okay, great, just making sure. I am Jocelyn Milner and I start working here on Monday. I was told to give you this."

I passed her the vanilla envelope and she took it, a confused expression overtaking her face.

"Alright," she said slowly. "I will see that these documents get to HR, but I didn't know there were any new positions open in the administrative department. Daniel is the hiring manager and he said they were overstaffed as is. "

"Oh, I won't be working in the administrative department. I was hired to manage the legal team."

"Who hired you?"

I didn't like her tone or the way her eyes narrowed at me. Explaining myself to her wasn't necessary, but it was also no secret since I would be working here and likely cross paths with her again.

"I'm sure you know them, Merrick Alexander and Ashton..." I paused to think about it, "Kent, I believe."

If I thought she was kind earlier, my brief assessment was inaccurate. The way she switched off the friendly and brought forth the fierce almost gave me whiplash.

"Of course, I know who Mr. Alexander and Mr. Kent are. Everyone does. They are the CEOs of Dual. Do you think I don't know who I work for?"

Well now. Looks like little Amber was a nut case, but she

would have to play psycho-girl games with someone else because I wasn't interested.

"Could you point me in the direction of Merrick's office, please?"

"Mr. Alexander," she said as if scolding me for addressing Merrick by his first name. "Is in a meeting with Mr. Kent and they do not like to be disturbed."

I counted to five before I spoke again.

"Either you tell me where Merrick's office is, or I will find it myself. And when I do, I will be sure to tell him how very unamiable you were."

I said it with a fake smile. A professional combo of nice and nasty was always my preference for dealing with impertinent people.

Amber repeated the word to herself and once again narrowed her eyes at me. I could tell she had no idea what the word meant.

Snatching up the phone receiver on her desk Amber pursed her lips and said with a sneer, "I will just check with Mr. Alexander."

Has Merrick slept with her? Or is this an innocent crush? I wondered.

Regardless, her territorial reaction clearly had nothing to do with business. After waiting a few seconds, Amber began to speak. I witnessed her crazy flip over to charming firsthand. The girl should be an actress.

"Mr. Alexander, I deeply apologize for disturbing you. I know how you hate to be interrupted during meetings," she said, giving me a cold glare, "but I have a woman here who is insisting I bother you."

She was a real piece of work.

I took pleasure in watching her face change as her contemptuous attitude was corrected. By the end of the phone call not only did she tell me where Merrick's office was located, but she also walked me there herself.

Entering Merrick's office, I was pleasantly surprised to see yet another handsome man. This one had enchanting hazel eyes and a heartwarming smile. He extended his hand to me.

"Welcome to the team, Jocelyn. I'm Ashton. It's nice to meet you."

Wow! Were all Merrick's friends/associates this hot? First, Xavier, and now Ashton. Maybe I could find a single one for Jada.

For now, I pushed that thought aside.

"It's nice to meet you as well. I am very excited to begin working and learning more about the company."

"We were just finishing up," Merrick said. "Please take a seat."

I sat in a comfortable, considerably large chair on wheels in front of Merrick's desk, while my two new bosses finished their meeting.

This office was huge. Probably the biggest I had ever seen and the floor-to-ceiling windows that displayed the view of the city were to die for.

Five minutes later, Ashton left, and Merrick went behind his desk and took a seat.

"Are you good?" he asked.

"Great!" I passed him the black folder and sat back down. "Your office is gigantic and I love the view."

"Thank you. Dual built the building, and I think we chose the location well, but if you think my office is nice, you should see Ashton's. It even has a fireplace."

My eyes widened. "Seriously?! That's a new one."

"Yup."

"Did you not want a fireplace?"

"Not really. It would have been a waste of space. Ashton is in the office a lot more than me handling new contracts and taking meetings. I conduct most of my business at home. Plus, I travel often to meet clients face to face."

I nodded in understanding.

"Are you sure Ashton knows about both parts of my position?" I asked in a whisper as if the man was still in the room.

"Trust me, he knows."

"And his... umm... sub works here?"

Merrick smiled. "You already asked that earlier, beautiful."

"I know, but... this is all so weird."

Merrick gave me a patient smile. "Yes, Jocelyn, he knows and he is fine with it. As far as her being a sub... I'm not sure."

"But I thought you said..." my voice trailed off.

"I said Ashton has his own arrangement. I didn't say she was a sub. I don't even know if Ashton is a Dom. As far as I know, he has never been part of the BDSM community. He simply enjoys submissive women."

I was confused.

"Isn't Ashton your best friend?"

Merrick laughed. "Yes, but I don't know the ends and outs of his sex life or his contracts. We are not women. Spending hours sharing the details of our deepest secrets is not what we do."

"All women don't do that!" I blurted, not even sure why because in my case he was correct. As soon as I got the chance I would be spilling this to Jada over a movie and ice cream.

Maybe I simply didn't like being called out.

He lifted his hands. "You are right. I retract my statement. Is there anything else you care to discuss?"

"Did you know your receptionist is a psycho?"

Merrick leaned back in his chair, placing his hands behind his head.

"Based on the few run-ins she has had with some staff members, I've heard Amber can be challenging."

Only a few? I thought to myself. *That's a surprise.*

"So why keep her around?" I asked, genuinely curious.

I didn't want the girl to get fired or reprimanded for anything, at least not because of me. I could handle her just fine.

"She was Ashton's hire. I think she's the daughter of a good friend of his, but besides that, her rating with the clients is off the charts and she does her job well."

"Gotcha, she is a brilliant psycho."

"Did she give you any trouble?" he asked.

I sat back and crossed my legs. "No."

Merrick opened his side desk drawer, then regarded me intently.

"Lying to me is another form of disrespect that I don't tolerate, but rather than call you out on it, I will only say this... You have been warned."

"I understand, sir," I said.

My eyes darted away from his. After the stuff I'd seen at the club the other night, I didn't know if I could withstand one of his punishments.

Too late now. You already signed the contract, my inner voice reminded me.

I thought I was only coming in here for a quick "We look forward to working with you" speech, but from the way Merrick was looking at me, I guess he had different plans.

"Would you still like to use the same safe word from the night at the club?" he asked.

I swallowed hard. "Yes, sir, red rose."

He gave me a curt nod.

"Do not forget it," he cautioned, pulling out four short

black ropes from the open drawer. My usual adventurous and carefree mindset did nothing to ease the bundle of nerves I'd just become. "Are you certain you're ready for this, Jocelyn?" he asked.

My voice had left me, so I only nodded, racking my brain to figure out what he was about to do.

Not taking his eyes off me, Merrick hit a button on his desk phone and said, "Amber, hold all my calls, please."

I shifted in my seat, and two words came to mind: *Oh. Shit.*

"Of course, Mr. Alexander," came Amber's perky reply.

Merrick stood and picked up the ropes. I stood too. I had no idea why or what I was thinking. I guess the sudden realization of exactly what I had gotten myself into had hit me.

"Sit down," he ordered.

I instantly complied.

Merrick moved around his desk and quietly circled my chair. I stared straight ahead. Those black ropes he was holding were occupying my thoughts.

Was he about to repeat what he had done at the club, bring me close to orgasm, then deny my release?

If so, I wouldn't be able to take it, which meant I was about to earn my first punishment.

Once he is in front of me again, he leans down. I assume he is about to kiss me, but instead, he puts his hand under the chair and raises it a little.

"Stand up," he said.

Before my feet could fully find the floor, he spun me around and guided me back into the chair—this time with my knees on the seat and my hands gripping the backrest.

"This is the same concept as the chair bondage technique I did at the club, but in reverse," he said, tying the first rope around my ankle, then connecting it to the lower half of the arm rail.

The rope was softer than I expected, never biting into my skin, but despite its plush feel, it cinched tight, leaving no room to move.

Merrick circled the chair and crouched, disappearing behind its tall back. He took my right wrist and secured it to the chair leg. A few seconds later, he did the same with my left.

It dawned on me that Merrick always explained how he planned to bind me. I'm not sure why, but knowing what came next eased my nerves, making it far easier to surrender my control.

The placement of the ropes had my hands lower than my ankles, causing a forced arch in my back. Turning my head to the side so that my cheek rested against the soft leather revealed a peripheral view of my ass high up in the air.

Merrick strolled back around the chair and skated his fingers along my hips, down my skirt, and the sides of my spread legs. He then pulled up my skirt, bunching it around my waist.

I am once again wearing no underwear and he grips my pussy with one large hand, coating his fingers with my juices and aggressively pressing his thumb against my clit.

I sucked in a sharp breath and clutched the legs of the chair with my bound hands.

The smile in his voice was evident when he said, "No underwear again, I see," I tried my hardest to remain quiet as he worked one, two, and then three fingers into me. "Tell me, Jocelyn, why do you not wear underwear?"

Feels better without it," I said, already lost to the delicious sensation of his fingers working inside me.

Merrick teased me for a few more minutes before finally withdrawing his hand. Then came the low, unmistakable sounds of his belt buckle loosening and his zipper sliding down. Reaching forward, he adjusted the chair, lifting it as high as it would go.

"That's what you tell yourself," he said, now teasing my entrance with the head of his dick. "But I think it's because you like men to have easy access to you. And that's what makes you the perfect slut."

I moaned as he sank his dick into me gradually, pulling the chair closer and closer until he was all the way in. I fought to keep my sounds of ecstasy to a minimum.

I hadn't even officially started the job yet. I wouldn't want to get fired.

Merrick took his time, lazily fucking me for what felt like ten blissful minutes, pushing me higher and higher until I was floating somewhere near cloud nine.

He rolled the chair back and forth, his dick sliding in and out of me, drawing louder, needier moans from my throat.

I assumed this was how it would go, an unbroken rhythm of slow, sensual thrusts, carrying me straight to an inevitable, delicious unraveling.

Clearly, I was wrong because Merrick suddenly pushed the chair up against a nearby wall and got down to business. There was no more light and easy; his thrusts were now rough and hard.

I enjoyed the switch-up.

"Do you feel that?" Merrick asked, his strong hands holding my waist firmly in place.

"Yes, sir... I... I do," I said, my words unsteady as I melted into the feeling, surrendering completely to the pleasure.

"Good," he replied, his voice hard with authority. "That's me claiming ownership of your body. You'll do what I want, when I want, and your only purpose is to keep me satisfied."

He buried one of his hands in my hair and pulled hard, forcing the upper half of my body back while his thrusts pushed the lower half of my body forward.

The ropes squeezed my limbs but still didn't break their

hold, and my pleas for more got me exactly what I wanted. Merrick fucked me harder.

"How does that feel, slut?" he asked, his dick digging deep into my pussy.

"Good sir, so good," I cried.

I wanted him to keep going. I needed him to keep going. Even if he broke me in two, the destruction of my body would be well worth it.

The earth-shattering capabilities of my impending orgasm were all promise and no illusion, and I wanted it.

"I bet it does," he said. "Because this is all you've ever wanted and you know what?" he leaned close to whisper his next words in my ear. "This is all you're good for."

Those words... that voice... his dominance. Oh shit. I was about to cum, but before I did, Merrick's rules resurfaced as if they had always been ingrained in me.

"Permission to cum, please, sir," I begged.

Merrick didn't respond and for a terrifying few seconds, I feared he didn't hear me. I held my breath, unable to do much else to try and stall my climax.

Finally, quietly and calmly, in that voice that made me weak, he said, "Yes, you may cum."

The eruption of my orgasm was ferocious. I trembled, bucked against the restraints, and screamed so loud Merrick had to cover my mouth.

His release came moments later, and he buried himself deep, while my pussy spasmed and tightened around his dick.

Once my shaking ended and I settled back into the here and now, Merrick untied me and I went to his personal bathroom to get cleaned up.

On my way out, things felt awkward. I didn't know what I was expected to do or say. *Should I simply leave? Or wait for him to dismiss me?*

I walked over to his desk, where he was leaning back in his

chair, flipping through a folder and talking to someone through his desk phone speaker.

Was that... Amber?

"Is everything okay, Mr. Alexander? I heard a scream coming from your office."

"Yes. Ms. Milner fell that's all."

Yeah, I fell alright, and landed on his dick, I thought mischievously.

I heard the fake concern in Amber's reply when she said, "Oh no! I hope she didn't hurt herself too badly."

Merrick assured her I was fine and ended the call.

He looked up at me and smiled.

"You're a screamer."

I briefly looked away, unsure of what to say about this recent discovery. Merrick was the only man who conjured that reaction out of me. I was never a screamer before.

You also weren't a submissive before, I reminded myself.

The thought made me remember that manners were important in this role, and since I hadn't thanked him yet for giving me an orgasm so strong I thought it would kill me, I said, "Thank you, sir. Is there anything else I can do for you?"

Merrick stared at me for a moment as if considering the question. Then he turned his attention back to the folder and said, "No, you've served your purpose for today. You're free to go. See you Monday."

I smiled to myself. This agreement was exactly what I wanted. No uncomfortable silences, messy emotions, or unrealistic expectations.

Just pure, aggressive, fulfilling, mind-numbing sex, a.k.a. my dream come true.

Once I made it to the door, Merrick called out to me, "Next time, Jocelyn," he said, closing the folder and tossing it into a bin on his desk, "I won't be so gentle."

Chapter Seven

"WHY DO I NEED NIPPLE CLAMPS?"

"Mom you have two appointments on Thursday and I already ordered your new medicine."

I put my car in park and checked my reflection in the mirror. It had been a long day, and the effortless curls I spent an hour styling this morning were being very disrespectful by looking like I hadn't put in any effort at all.

"Jocelyn, you have already reminded me about the appointment, and thank you for the medicine I won't forget to take them."

"Mom," I said in an admonishing tone.

"I know, I know. I forgot to take them last time, but I'm going to do better. I give you my word."

She always gave me her word. Promising me that she would do better at taking care of herself, but she was always so busy taking care of everyone else, she often left herself for last or out completely.

"I worry about you, mom, that's all."

"Why, sweetie?" my mom said, her gentle voice bringing back fond childhood memories. "I'm fine. Your father has been so kind lately. You have nothing to worry about."

That ruined my special moment of memories.

"Gary is not my father. My father died when I was seventeen, remember?"

My mom exhaled. She wanted me to accept Gary and form some unbreakable bond. But if it hadn't happened in ten years, it wasn't going to happen. Plus, it was hard to construct some deep connection with a man who often lashed out when angry.

"I know he has his faults, but he has been a father to you."

I kept my mouth shut. She always took up for him. Through the abuse, the lies, and the cheating. I had no idea what type of hold he had over her, but it didn't work on me. I saw Gary for what he was, a piece of shit.

"How's Ginger?" I asked, changing the subject.

Ginger was my mom's close friend who had recently moved to a senior citizen community.

My mom's voice perked up.

"Ginger is great! I went to see her Saturday and played bingo with her and some of her neighbors. I even won a prize!"

"That's wonderful, mom. What did you win?"

"Twenty-five dollars and next week the prize is a big screen TV. I plan on winning that prize as well," she announced confidently.

Her excitement filled my heart with joy.

When my mom experienced stress or failed to care for herself, her illness worsened. However, when things were going well, she truly thrived.

The problem was as long as Gary was around, who knew how long her good times would last?

"I am so happy you are taking time out for yourself."

"Me too! Two weeks ago I'd been feeling really weak, but the past few days I've had the energy of a newborn. I might even start taking swimming lessons and hanging out all night."

"Look at you," I teased. "Am I going to have to set a curfew for you?"

"Oh, hush," she replied with a laugh. "Enough about me. What's going on with you? Are you enjoying your new job?"

More than I should, I thought to myself.

But before I could give her an appropriate response, I heard Gary's husky voice in the background.

"Joann! I'm hungry. Where is dinner?"

"I'll start on it in a minute," my mom said. "I'm talking to Jocelyn right now, honey."

"I'll bet she had dinner already," was his snappy response.

I heard rumbling and movement. I assumed my mom was trying to cover the phone so that I didn't hear his rude retort.

"Your father said hello," she lied.

I cringed. That asshat didn't deserve that title.

"Tell him, hi," I said, choosing to go along with the story for her sake.

"Now, what were you saying, sweetie?" she asked.

I started again. "Work is going—"

"Joann!" Gary shouted, cutting me off. "How much longer?"

"Jocelyn," my Mom said. I could hear the plea in her voice.

"It's okay, Mom. Go ahead, I can talk to you later."

"I promise I will call you back as soon as I can," she said.

"Don't stress yourself, Mom. We will talk soon. Have fun at Bingo," I replied, feigning a joy I didn't feel.

We said our goodbyes and I glanced at the clock.

Darn it! I was late, and being late broke one of the rules.

I was supposed to meet Merrick at 7 and it was already 7:02. Add in the three minutes it took for me to get inside and for the hostess to show me to the table where Merrick awaited me, and I officially arrived at 7:05.

I know because I discreetly checked my watch.

Merrick was holding his phone to his ear, a serious expression on his face. As soon as he saw me, his entire mood seemed to brighten. I tried not to read too much into it, but the warm feeling it gave me didn't go unnoticed.

"I have to go, Jocelyn has arrived," he said, ending the call.

Merrick stood, kissed me on the cheek, and pulled out my chair for me.

His manners were definitely one of the most attractive things about him.

"Thank you," I said. "Sorry, I'm late."

"No problem. How was the drive? Any issues?"

"Nope, no issues."

Taking his seat again, Merrick called over the waiter to get us started with some water before speaking again.

"Tell me, how was your first official week?"

I placed my hands to my heart and exhaled with exuberance.

"Amazing! Very busy, as you already know, but I truly enjoy the work. The cases are straightforward, nothing I am unfamiliar with and the legal team is the best."

"That's wonderful. I noticed you got Stonewall Supplies to concede. The way you wrote that cease and desist letter was ingenious. We had been working on that one for months with barely any progress."

"It was no big deal," I said, brushing off the recognition.

"It is a big deal," Merrick insisted. "I don't think we could have done that without you. At least not so efficiently and effectively. Your intelligence and legal skills are extraordinary. Don't ever downplay your value."

I had no idea what to say. The level of respect and admiration in his voice moved me.

"Thank you," I said with a smile, then catching a glimpse at the menu, it dawned on me that I didn't see my purse. I glanced around, making sure it hadn't fallen on the floor.

"What are you looking for?"

"My purse. I thought I brought it inside, but maybe I left it in the car."

"You don't need that."

I did a final check underneath my chair, the search

requiring me to hang upside down briefly. At this point, surely my effortless curls were so messy they made me look like a lunatic.

"Yes, I do. I am going to need my wallet to pay for my dinner."

"I am paying for your dinner."

"That's sweet, but there is no need. I got it."

"I didn't ask if you had it." I looked up at him. His gaze was non-negotiable. "When you are with me, you don't pay for anything, you don't open any doors and you do what you are told."

There was that authority again.

"I understand, sir. Thank you."

"What are you thinking about ordering?" he asked.

"I'm not sure," I replied, checking out the menu. This was a Malaysian restaurant and everything looked so good. "What about you?"

"Possibly the Ikan Bakar."

I located it on the menu. It was a grilled fish Marinated with turmeric, ginger, galangal, chili, garlic and fresh lime. I lowered my menu and glanced up at him.

"Do you eat junk food?"

Merrick laughed. "That was out of left field. Why do you ask?"

"I don't know. Your meal choices always seem so healthy, and now I wonder if that's because you are some health nut who avoids starches and sweets?"

"You're sweet and I had no issues eating you." A warmth rushed over me. "However, to answer your question, beyond feasting on you, no, I don't eat junk food."

The waiter came over again, this time to take our orders, but Merrick dismissed him and said we needed more time. I stared at him confused. I thought he would be ready to eat, but more time did sound good. I was still trying to decide between beef, chicken, or lamb to go with my rice cooked in coconut milk.

"Now, that the basics are out of the way," Merrick said, "let's deal with your punishment."

My head snapped up. "Punishment?"

"You were five minutes late."

"Okay, yeah, but that's only five minutes. You know that I am always on time for everything. For work, I even arrive an hour early."

"And yet..." he said with a light shrug, "you were late today. I told you one of my rules is to never be late for an appointment with me."

"But it's only five minutes!" I exclaimed again.

"I don't care if it were five seconds. Late is late," he said pointedly. "Would you like to share the reason for your delay? Maybe I will take it into consideration."

I thought about my mom and the issues with Gary. Those wounds cut deep and I was not interested in sharing that with him. Plus, it would blur the lines between professional and personal, and I didn't want his pity.

"Give me your best shot, sir," I said with a smile.

"I knew you would say that. Your punishment is dessert before dinner." My brows furrowed, but Merrick's statement was clarified by what he said next. "I need to release some tension and you are going to take care of it."

"Mmm," I hummed. "A blowjob before dinner? I'm game for that. Should I sneak off to the bathroom first and you follow me?"

"No, you will do it here."

I blinked a few times and looked around. "At the table?"

"Is that a problem?"

I glanced down. The tablecloth was black, pleated, thick, and stretched all the way down to the floor.

"No, sir. There is no problem."

"Good."

"So just do it?" I whispered. "Maybe I should knock something down on the floor so that ducking underneath the cloth looks less suspicious."

"Whatever gets you on your knees," he replied indifferently. "But there are rules."

"Rules?" I repeated, my stomach tightening.

"Yes. If your hands aren't on my dick, then they should be on my legs. Do not touch yourself. This is for my benefit, not yours."

This was not like the night at the club. That show was for people who were in on the kink. They didn't judge and they wouldn't kick me out for lewd behavior; a restaurant was a different ball game.

Merrick reached into his suit jacket and pulled out a small black box. Placing it on the table, he slides it over to me.

"Put these on."

A sudden spike of adrenaline filled me.

Was this jewelry? Couldn't be.

Inside I found a long sparkly, gold, and pink chain. I lifted it from its velvet case and twirled it from side to side. It had to have been at least eighteen inches long and a closer examination revealed two clamps on either end with small diamonds embedded in them.

"What is it?"

"Nipple clamps."

They definitely looked expensive and glistened in the light.

"Okay," I said slowly. "You expect me to wear these?"

"I do, and you will," Merrick said.

I looked down at my white button-up blouse.

If I undid a few buttons, I could easily... No! Hell no! I wasn't wearing these.

I lowered the glamorous torture chains back into the box.

Shaking my head, I said, "I don't think I can wear these."

Merrick leaned forward, a warning tone in his voice. "Are you denying my request?"

My eyes drifted back down to the clamps again. I wasn't trying to deny it, but damn, what if it hurts?

"No, sir, I'm just scared it may hurt."

"If it does you deserve it."

I swallowed audibly. "With all due respect... sir," I said, adding the title after I noticed how his eyes narrowed at me. "Why do you even want me to wear them? I can suck your dick without accessories."

"It's not for you. It's for me. I will use it to direct you. I want you to go underneath the table, put them on and pass the chain to me. When you are going too fast, I will let you know. Too slow, I will do the same, and maybe just for fun..." he sat back and smirked. "Well, you get it."

My heart pounded wildly in my chest. This was my first official punishment as a submissive and it surpassed anything in my wildest imagination.

Could I do this? Would I do this? Should I do this?

"Don't let my relaxed demeanor fool you, Jocelyn. You've got three seconds to obey my request before you earn an additional punishment," Merrick said.

Releasing a lengthy sigh, I removed my feet from my heels and picked up the clamps.

Time to put your money where your mouth is... or in this case.... Merrick's dick, where your mouth is, I decided.

"Yes, sir," I said, committing to his request.

Discretely, I slid down and lifted the heavy black fabric, disappearing underneath. Once I was completely hidden, I looked around and waited. For what, I'm not sure.

Perhaps I assumed the waitress would peek underneath and say, *"Ha! I saw you. What are you doing down there?"*

But nothing happened.

The tablecloth was only a few inches from touching the floor, which meant if someone looked hard enough, they might see slightly indistinguishable movements at the bottom of the table.

I let out another long breath, trying to gear myself up.

You know you want to, the naughtier side of me urged.

Closing my eyes, I thought about how good he tasted that first night and felt my mouth water. My arousal was finally starting to outweigh my indecision.

The longer you wait, the higher your chances of being seen, my logical half reminded me.

I stared up at the bottom half of Merrick and even that limited view of him was titillating. His nicely fitted black slacks showcased powerful thighs and a thick bulge in his pants, encouraging me to begin.

He had one hand underneath the table, tapping his leg, patiently waiting.

Note to self: make sure Merrick doesn't practice witchcraft.

The pull he had over me was beginning to raise my suspicions.

I glanced down at the chain fisted in my hand. It might have been made for impish torture, but it was still stunning. I made fast work of undoing the buttons on my shirt, then I folded down the padding of my bra to uncover my breasts.

Holding my nipple between my thumb and forefinger, I squeezed my eyes shut and applied the first clamp, waiting for the spike of pain to rush in and torment me. I was utterly dumbfounded when it didn't happen.

The pinching sensation actually felt good and added to the excitement of this improper act. I quickly applied the second clamp and crawled over to him.

Rubbing my hands over his thighs to let him know I was there, Merrick flipped his hand, palm up, silently requesting the chain. I placed it in his hand and his fingers closed around it instantly.

Getting him off would require me to work fast and forgo my usual initial teasing methods. Therefore, after freeing his already erect dick, I spit on my hand and used that to get things started.

Stroking him for several seconds, I covered the head of his dick with my mouth and sucked, letting the thrill of such a scandalous act rush in and mentally whisk me away. I worked my tongue and throat up and down his hardness feeling it jerk in my mouth every time I tensed my lips around him.

The clatter and clang of utensils against plates and endless dinner chatter sounded all around me, but I barely noticed it. All those people were out there, and I was here, secluded and thirstily sucking the dick of a man I had consented to serve.

The first tug on the chain was unexpected but easy to decipher. Albeit I wasn't moving fast, I thought I was doing a pretty good job of taking all of him in.

However, it was apparent that Merrick wanted me to increase the pace. I moved my hand up and down, tightening my grip each time it traveled upward.

When I figured he'd had enough, I switched tactics – using my hand to stimulate only the lower half of his dick and my mouth to engulf the upper half.

I wasn't sure how much time passed, but I really got into it.

Underneath this table, there was no need to fret over my broken heart. I didn't have to be strong or endure struggles and pain for myself or anyone else. I could simply let go, submit to Merrick and go where the adventure took me.

Wanting this to be good for him, I sucked quicker and harder. I not only needed him to cum, but I had to finish this punishment before I was spotted.

Merrick yanked the chain again, and I gasped with his dick

still in my mouth. He must have loved that sensation because I felt his manhood throb.

Placing my palms on his thighs, I hiked up on my knees to deep-throat him. I felt liberated and so dirty that trickles of wetness saturated my inner thigh.

Then suddenly, I heard a voice that wasn't Merrick's and I froze. I felt like someone had smacked me back into reality and the fear of being discovered made me withdraw him from my mouth.

I tried to sit back on my heels, but with him holding my nipples hostage with that damn chain, I had to settle for hovering near his lap.

"I came to refill your waters and see if you were ready for me to take your orders, but I see your dinner companion isn't here."

Merrick tugged on the chain... hard. He obviously wanted me to get back to my punishment, but I didn't move.

"She had a work matter to take care of, but will be back shortly," Merrick replied.

His response to my disobedience was to become more aggressive.

Pulling the chain higher, he slipped it over his erection, and it slid down to rest at the base of his dick.

A sharp spike of complex sensations traveled through my breasts down to my pussy. I had to bite my lip to muffle the moan that escaped.

Who knew something could hurt and feel this good at the same time?

With renewed determination and no longer concerned with the waiter, I buried my face in Merrick's lap, greedily swallowing the length of him.

Every time I took him all the way down, my lips would repeatedly brush the chain resting at the base of his dick. A fierce heat kindled between my legs, tempting me to break the rules and touch myself.

As if he could read my mind, Merrick placed his hands over mine, pinning them to his legs. I don't know how I managed to finish him off without cumming myself, but I did.

His hands tensed over my own and spurts of his release filled my mouth. I downed it quickly, relaxing my tongue near the tip so that I could feel it stream out.

Finally, his breathing steadied, but his hands were still holding mine captive. I didn't know what else he wanted me to do, so I simply waited.

After a moment, Merrick reached out and removed the clamp from one of my nipples, and wow! My sensations were amplified unlike ever before. He massaged it gently as the blood rushed back to it, giving me bursts of euphoria.

A few seconds later, he did the same to the other and the result was equally enjoyable.

When he let me go, I buttoned up my shirt and cautiously got back into my seat. I looked around. No weird stares and the only eyes watching me belonged to Merrick.

"You might be one of the best subs I have ever had," he said. "How did you feel about your first punishment?"

I couldn't stop the smile from forming on my face.

"It was... exhilarating," I said honestly. "I can't believe I liked it so much!"

"That is good news for me."

"I guess it is," I said.

"And..." he urged. "Have you forgotten your manners already?"

I looked down sheepishly. "Sorry. Thank you, sir."

The gratitude aspect still felt a little foreign to me, but I understood its purpose. Thanking him or asking permission was my verbal way of cementing his control over me and that was what made this whole arrangement more riveting.

"Good girl. Oh, by the way," he said, his way of addressing me switching from authoritative to business. "I meant to tell you that Ashton is also thoroughly impressed with your work. He wanted me to tell you that, just in case..."

There was that mischievous grin again.

"In case what?" I asked.

"In case I wanted to reward you for it," he replied with a wink.

"You are hilarious," I said, shaking my head. "How do you even do that?"

"Do what?"

"Switch on and off so easily. One minute I'm an exceptional lawyer that you treat as your equal. The next, I'm a whore whose only purpose lies in being of service to you."

He grabbed my hand and laid a gentle kiss on it. My body quivered under the feel of his soft lips and enthralling touch.

"You are completely out of your element, aren't you?" he said.

"I am," I responded, owning up to my ignorance.

Merrick gave me an easy smile.

"You're both, Jocelyn."

That answer baffled me. "But how?" I said it aloud, but I wasn't really looking for him to answer.

The question was more so meant for myself, which is why I was surprised when he said, "You're a powerful woman. And many powerful women prefer someone else to be in control during sex. It allows you to be in the moment instead of trying to orchestrate it, which is a constant demand for you."

I could only listen and stare, wide-eyed and blown away, as this man I barely knew explained my perplexed emotions so simply.

"I have been a Dom for over eleven years and I have seen a lot. You are learning new things about yourself and your sexuality. It's normal to be confused, excited and even a little scared."

I couldn't have said it better myself. I liked where Merrick was taking me and couldn't wait to experience more. I ran my fingers teasingly over his hand and glanced down at the nipple clamps, my new favorite toy.

"How do you suggest I move forward, sir?" I asked playfully, already knowing what his answer would be.

"Simple. Trust me and do what you do best. I'll handle the rest."

"Yes, sir," I said, feeling more grounded already.

He motioned for the waiter to come over, then said, "Now, let's eat."

"Wait, so you're like a high-paid prostitute or something?" Jada asked in astonishment.

She sat on the floor painting her toenails while I stretched out on the couch with my computer resting on my lap.

"No," I responded, pointing a finger in her general vicinity. My eyes were glued to the computer screen as I attempted to make a payment towards my mom's electric bill. "I am a high-paid lawyer. As far as sex goes, it's free because I'm his submissive."

"What does that even mean?"

I grinned. "In short, whatever he wants it to mean."

Jada's hand darted to her mouth. "Jocelyn, are you saying you let this man do," her voice lowered," perverse things to you like tie you up? And call you names?"

"Yes, and oh, yes," I said, the thought made me wet. "But the only perverse things he does is what I allow."

I hit the green "pay" button and looked up from my computer. Jada's face was a mixture of confusion, terror and intrigue.

"I'm at a loss for words," she said. "Why would you even sign up for something like that?" Her brows were up so high they disappeared underneath her curly bangs and her nail polish brush hovered over her toes.

I thought about it, then shrugged.

"Why not? He and I are both single and extremely attractive might I add. Besides, there is no way I could work for Merrick and not sleep with him. I think it was a very mature move to skip the games."

"My best friend as an actual sub," Jada said, staring off into the distance to let it sink in. "No, no, no, it's not working. I can't picture it. It's too weird."

"Aww, come on, it's just sex. Is it weird when two co-workers hook up?" I asked.

Jada opened her mouth, closed it, opened it again, and then settled for giving me a steely glare.

"Don't try to confuse me!" Jada said. "No, sleeping with someone at the job isn't weird, but it's also different because that scenario happens organically. A contractual agreement for sex is... strange as hell."

"I like the contract. It makes things a lot less messy," I replied.

Jada leaned in. "Oh, I have to hear this. Please tell me how leasing out your pussy makes it less messy?"

I picked up a pillow from the couch and threw it at her. She dodged it and fell back, laughing on the floor. After we both got our laughter under control, Jada joined me on the couch, wobbling over on her heels to avoid ruining her toenails.

"I know you don't understand this, but Merrick and I set up this agreement because we want sex and nothing else. That works well for me because I don't have to worry about him becoming like Aaron or any other guy, trying to make me live out their marital dreams."

I left out the minor detail that Merrick was open to a relationship because that would only solidify her point that this was messy.

Jada snatched up her phone from the coffee table.

"I'm calling the psychiatric ward. You have officially lost it."

"No," I said, seizing it from her hand. "I think I've found it. All the sex I can handle with no drama and an amazing job. I've hit the lottery."

"You've hit your head if you don't think this spells disaster."

"I don't care if you think it spells delusional. To me, it spells dick, and Merrick's feels like riding a unicorn off into the sunset," I said, extending my hand up and outward with a mesmerized look in my eyes.

"But that proves my point of how insane this is. Unicorns aren't real."

"I'm not even sure Merrick is real. I have never met a man like him before."

Jada gripped my shoulders and shook me. "Wake up, Jocelyn. Are you sure about this?"

"My pussy is," I replied playfully.

"Jocelyn! I am serious."

"So am I. The paperwork has already been signed and taking risks doesn't scare me. If I lose this job. I'll find another."

She released me, eyeing me skeptically. "You are like a cat in that way. Always landing on your feet. But don't say I didn't tell you so."

"Don't worry. I won't."

Jada crossed her arms and an adorable grin spread across her face.

"Alright, so, tell me about it?"

I turned my attention back to my laptop. I had a few more bills to pay.

"You know, courtroom battles, meetings, litigations, clients trying to swindle their way out of fault or responsibility-"

"Not the legal position!" Jada interrupted. "The Sex!"

"But you don't approve so why do you want to hear about it?" I said with an enigmatic smile.

"Jocelyn Renee Milner. If you don't tell me the juicy details I will hurt you!"

"Look at you using my middle name. You must mean business, but I don't know the details may be too wild for you," I said teasingly. "You did say I'd lost my mind."

"You *have* lost your mind, but this arrangement sounds hella sexy."

I felt an immense sense of exuberance. "It really is."

Jada shook her head and gave me her most vicious side-eye, which I ignored since I was almost done taking care of my mom's household expenses.

"I can't believe you had the nerve to tell me that Merrick, the guy from your one-night stand, was only alright in bed. Now, I find out he was the best you ever had. You better spill it all!"

I laughed. "I lied okay, I didn't think I would ever see him again and didn't want to dwell on it."

"Whatever your reasonings," Jada replied with a wave of her hand, "I need to hear everything."

"Okay, but give me a second. I have to finish paying one last bill first."

Jada crossed her arms.

"This better be good since I have to wait."

I typed in the amount I wished to pay, hit the submit button, and placed my laptop on the table.

"Alright, imagine this, a restaurant, a blow job and... nipple clamps."

I dragged my finger across the line that stated the reason for the worker's compensation request and frowned.

This was the tenth claim Theodore Blakey had submitted this year. That was highly suspicious.

Even though the very nature of construction work came with plenty of safety risks, Dual was excellent about keeping their work sites under proper occupational safety and health standards, so why the excess claims from Blakey?

He was the only employee this year to file that many claims.

I glanced at my calendar. I was going to pencil in a few surprise visits to the worksite to ensure that proper protocols were being followed.

Paying employees due to unavoidable injuries was one thing, but if foul play was involved, the company was losing money and I intended to stop it.

A knock on the door disrupted my early investigation process.

"Come in," I called out.

The knob turned and in stepped Merrick.

I'd been working here for a month now and still, the mere sight of him always made my day brighter... or was that the sex?

No, it was definitely him. Merrick's aura was a stress reliever, add in the searing, soul-satisfying sex, and he became my walking addiction.

"Hi, are you busy?" he asked. "I know your caseload is heavy this week."

"It is, but I have a little time. What's up?"

He closed my door, locked it, then came to take a seat in

front of my desk. I did a little dance on the inside. Locking the door meant something scandalous was about to happen.

"I wanted to ask you about Theodore Blakey. Have you come across his file yet?" Merrick said.

I lifted the paper on my desk, "Funny, you should ask. I was reviewing it now."

"I was weighing the pros and cons of letting him go. What do you think?"

I chewed my bottom lip. "It may not be wise to jump the gun just yet. His repeated claims are suspicious, but I want to look into the medical reports for all of his incidents, including this latest one. If Blakey is guilty of negligence and/or making false claims, he will need to reimburse Dual."

"Why can't we simply fire him and figure it out later."

"You could, but legally speaking it's sloppy. Especially if he has probable cause for filing those claims. He could turn around and sue Dual."

"And see, that's why I always defer to you," he said charmingly. "Please keep me in the loop on your findings."

"Of course. Any other reason you stopped by?" I asked.

"There is. I am about to head out for seven days."

"Right, this is your travel week," I said, pretending as if I'd forgotten. The truth was, I'd been dreading this day ever since he told me about it two weeks ago.

"It is. I go to Miami for three days and then to California for another four."

"Sounds like a lot. Lucky for you, I bought you something."

He didn't even try to hide the surprise on his face.

"Really?!"

"Yup." I opened my drawer, pulled out a small black bag and passed it to him.

"I'm almost afraid to look. What is this?" he asked, opening the bag.

"Junk food," I said proudly. "Chips, peanuts, crackers (the very high sodium kind), and candy. I got you all the bad stuff."

Merrick lifted some chips from the bag, studied it, then dropped them back inside.

"Please tell me, what inspired you to get me junk food?"

"Because you said you don't eat it, but since I do, I figured it would give you something fun to remember me by."

He shook his head and smiled.

"I have never had a sub buy me junk food before. I am going to miss seeing you every day," he said, his flirting apparent.

I only gave him a playful grin. There was no way I would confess any of my emotions to him. Even though I would long for his company as well.

"Go ahead and admit it. You're going to miss seeing me, too, aren't you? It's written all over your face."

"I am going to miss seeing certain parts of you," I said casually.

He laughed. "And that! How can I go a whole week without your snappy comebacks?"

"I could always text them to you late at night when I am touching myself."

His jovial tone vanished so quickly that I had to look up to make sure I wasn't talking to a different person.

"If you touch yourself while I'm gone, the last punishment I gave you will look like a walk in the park."

I cleared my throat, turned on and disturbed at what that would look like.

"Yes sir, no self-play."

I was going to commit to it but wasn't certain I could pull it off. I watched his eyes fully transition from playful to predatory.

Oh yeah, here we go. I am about to get some action.

"Clear off your desk," Merrick instructed. "Leave only your computer and phone."

I dropped the pen I was holding and began clearing the few items from my desk.

A stack of folders, some light paperwork, and a cup filled with pens, pencils, and scissors, were all placed on a nearby table.

"Lie on your back across the desk, letting your head hang over the edge," he quietly ordered.

I did as told, and Merrick walked around the desk, stopping a foot in front of my face. When he began to unhook his belt, I felt flustered all over. He was about to fuck my mouth right here in my office.

Yum.

I couldn't help but notice that even upside down he was sexy.

Merrick traced his dick over my lips, coating them with his precum. I imagined from his point of view that I looked like a woman with a fresh coat of shiny lip gloss.

He admired his handy work for several seconds before saying, "Open your mouth."

I licked my lips in anticipation.

Welp, there goes my cum flavored lip gloss.

After following his orders, Merrick inserted himself swiftly, pushing so hard that I had to grab the edges of the desk to hold myself in place. Once his desired rhythm for my throat fucking had been determined, I firmly planted my hands on either side of my body.

When Merrick used me to get himself off, he wanted zero interference from me. My assignment was always the same; follow orders and enjoy being of service.

He began toying with my shirt, loosening one button each time he shifted forward until my blouse was completely open.

He took his time running his hands over my stomach and sides before massaging my breast through my bra.

I loved the way his touch ignited me and brought my senses to life. All at once, I could hear the wet sounds of his dick drilling into my mouth, feel the soft brushes and pinches of his fingers teasing my skin and smell his inviting masculine scent.

Moving his hands underneath my bra, he tugged aggressively on my already hard nipples. I arched my back, wanting more. He obliged, squeezing and twisting them to the point of pain and I reveled in his unrestraint.

Once I entered this zone, I didn't care what he did to me. I willingly renounced all of my control because giving him what he wanted gave me what I needed; to be mentally free from stress and worry.

His thrusts were now coming so fast that the back of my head was pinned firmly against the edge of the desk.

"Your obedience will be rewarded soon," Merrick promised, which meant he was getting close.

Out of my peripheral, I noticed him pull the pair of scissors from the cup I had placed on a nearby table, but within seconds, it was out of sight.

The angle of my head prevented me from seeing what he was doing. But, judging by the sudden upward pull on my bra, I was fairly certain I knew what was coming next.

Is he really about to do this?

If so, I felt no fear, but my pussy felt fantastic. It had practically melted into a puddle underneath me. This was so fucking hot. I wanted desperately to catch a peek and watch him cut it, but this damn viewpoint was obstructive.

I heard the scissors slice through the lacy fabric, felt the bra give way and the air in the room caressed my exposed chest. Merrick dropped the scissors on the floor and wrapped a hand around each breast, using them to anchor him as his orgasm broke free.

I devoured it, hating when the spurts slowed, and he eventually finished. Pulling himself from my mouth, I noticed a few droplets of cum still covering the head of his dick. I stared at it and then up at him, awaiting his permission.

"Go ahead and clean it up."

"Thank you, sir," I said.

I rolled over to my stomach and licked the residual cum off. I took my precious time to savor it and squeezed him tighter just in case there was more. A few drops squirted out and just like the good girl he always said I was, I consumed it greedily.

Five minutes later, I stood in front of him, rubbing the back of my neck. I guess I hadn't noticed at the time, but the desk dug into it pretty hard. Merrick removed my hand and replaced it with his, massaging the tender area.

"Are you okay?" he asked.

"I am."

It wasn't a lie. My head really didn't hurt that bad. And now that I'd had a taste, I wanted him to be rougher.

What was happening to me?

"Being a submissive isn't always going to be comfortable, but don't forget to use your safe word or another form of communication if it ever becomes too much."

My eyes found his.

"There was no need for that because I liked it."

I looked down at my still-exposed breasts. My bra had been sliced in half, rendering it useless and my erect nipples pointed straight out, begging for more attention.

"What should I do about the fact that I have no bra?"

Merrick stopped caressing the back of my head and relocated his hand to my breast, rubbing his thumb over one of the sensitive beads.

"I don't know, that's your problem." Then a wicked smile crossed his lips and he added, "I got what I came for."

Those were the words I said to him the first night we met after he asked me if I would tell him my name. I was surprised he remembered my words and even more impressed that he would use them against me.

A low moan escaped my lips.

"I understand, sir. I'll figure it out."

"See that you do," he said, "but in the meantime, you are welcome to use the company card under my account to replace it."

He released my nipple and I whimpered. I didn't want this to end.

He tilted my chin upward. "Alright, gorgeous, I need to leave before I miss my flight. You were amazing as usual."

"Thank you for allowing me to please you before you left, sir."

"And why wouldn't I? Isn't that what whores are for?"

Something stirred inside me and I bit my lip. Merrick knew how turned on I already was. His use of degrading words only made matters worse.

"I love when you call me that."

"Call you what?" he said, forcing me to say it.

There was no shame in it for me. "A whore," I said boldly.

"Isn't that what you are?"

"Yes, sir."

"Good, and you better not forget it."

My eyes found his. Suddenly I didn't give a damn about his flight time or schedule. He was going to fuck me. I would make sure of it.

He'd warned me before to never test him or break the rules on respect. However, seven days without him and being forbidden to touch myself was about to cause his dominant side to meet mine.

I stepped closer to him. My bare breasts pressed hard against his chest.

"If you want me to heed that warning, do me a favor and point me in the direction of a Dom that knows how to show this whore who is boss. Because I'm not sure that you can."

He was on me before I could take my next breath, ripping my shirt and what was left of my bra off my body and discarding it on the floor. One strong hand was around my neck, pinning me flat against my desk and the other forced my legs to spread wide.

Since I had a habit of not wearing any underwear, Merrick had easy access to enter me. Without hesitation, his dick impaled my pussy in a motion so fast I didn't visually catch it but wholeheartedly felt it.

It was glorious and highly intoxicating.

His hand tightened around my neck, reducing my air supply to a dangerously low level, and that caused heightened sensations of my impending orgasm to ricochet through me.

I saw stars and had evidently pulled something out of him that was savage and remorseless. It fed some deep yearning desire that hid deep inside me.

I wrapped my legs around him, wanting every inch, every aggression and every malicious intent Merrick had to give.

I came hard. My body convulsed as my mood oscillated from tense to extreme delectation. Merrick's explosion came shortly thereafter, but instead of filling my body with his release, he pulled out and unloaded himself onto my heaving chest.

Using one finger, he swiped up some cum that landed on my nipple and brought it to my lips.

"Open your fucking mouth," he ordered.

I did, still quivering in delight as I proceeded to suck the creamy, warm release from his finger.

His eyes were fueled with something I had never seen before and if I'm being honest, something I hoped to see again.

"Make no mistake, Jocelyn," he said, twisting his finger slowly inside my mouth. "I will always treat you like the whore that you are. But challenge my authority again and not only will I fuck you until you can no longer stand, but once you fall to your knees, I will chain you to the wall where you will spend an entire weekend swallowing my cum for breakfast, lunch and dinner."

Then, leaving me on my desk satiated and shirtless, with my breasts covered in his sticky release, Merrick left my office, not sparing me a second glance.

I think I'm in love.

Chapter Nine

A week later, I nervously walked up the five stairs that led to Merrick's front door. Less than an hour ago, I'd been at my desk working yet another late Friday evening when my cell rang.

Long story short, Merrick called, I came... and hopefully, by the end of the night, I would be cumming a whole lot more.

I was actually blown away by the fact that he had invited me here. At the beginning of all this, he said I'd have to earn it. I guess that meant I had, by doing what, I had no idea.

The last time I saw him, he was exiting my office to catch a flight, and besides texts about business, I hadn't spoken to him since.

I pressed the doorbell and waited... nothing. After a full minute passed, I pushed it again, and still... nothing.

Once five minutes had gone by, I opened my purse to pull out my phone, but there was no need. The door swung open, and there he stood – the man of all my day, night, and wet dreams.

He was shirtless, in jeans, with a towel tossed over his shoulders. My body exploded in tingles and sensations the second I laid eyes on him.

Damn my raging and weak hormones! I got wet off the mere sight of this man. I had to do better.

But how?

With that face and those exquisitely toned v-cut abs that disappeared into his jeans, I felt like I was standing in front of a calendar model being photographed coming out of the ocean.

I circled back to the arousal he elicited in me, noticing for the first time that he was wet, too, well, his chest and hair were.

"I apologize for the delay," Merrick said. "I had a meeting run late and just got out of the shower. Please come in."

He stepped aside, and I entered his oversized lavish home. It was nothing less than what I expected. Judging from the impeccable landscape and the stone and brick custom designs of the homes themselves, I suspected not one house in this community cost less than several million dollars.

I stood in a spacious open concept that combined the living room, kitchen, and dining area. Bright walls, luxurious furniture, soft jazz playing in the background and the smell of something delicious surrounded me.

I really need to stop skipping lunch.

Merrick walked to the right towards the kitchen and I remained standing by the front door. I considered it rude to roam around without his permission, and simply following behind him made me feel like a lost puppy.

He returned a minute later holding two glasses of wine.

"Why are you just standing there?" he asked, nodding towards the couch, "Make yourself at home."

We sat on a navy blue sofa that turned out to be quite comfortable. That realization surprised me. Usually, expensive-looking furniture made me feel like I was sitting on cardboard.

"Jazz and a glass of wine are my go-to's for winding down," I said. "You've got good taste."

Merrick watched me carefully before replying. "I chose you, so I would have to agree."

As usual, I ignored his come-on by getting the attention off of me.

"I love your home. How long have you lived here?"

"Three years, but I am thinking of downsizing. This is entirely too much space for me. I got it when I thought my aunt and uncle would need to move in. They are older and didn't want to live on their own."

"Oh," I said, touched by his generosity. "What happened?"

"We all decided that my cousin's place was a better fit. I travel often, and being alone for too long makes them nervous."

"I understand that," I said, thinking about my mom.

Was that why she put up with Gary?

"Anyway," Merrick said, placing a glass of wine in my hand, "how was your day?"

He was still shirtless, except now the towel was gone, and I could easily smell his fresh body wash.

"It was fine. How was yours?"

Merrick scrubbed a hand over his face and took a large gulp of wine.

"It was long. Too long. I'm grateful it's Friday. I plan to take the weekend off. What about you?"

"Nothing much on my end. My only plans are to chill, relax..." I almost added, *"and worry myself to death,"* but closed my mouth.

Unfortunately, issues with my mom had been breaking my concentration all day. She called me around noon to tell me that she wasn't feeling well and was headed to the hospital. Both she and I figured her new meds were to blame, but the doctor would check her out to be sure.

I thought Gary must have been taking her, but when she

mentioned not forgetting money to pay the uber driver, I learned that Gary wasn't even home.

He got drunk at a friend's house the night before playing poker and she hadn't heard from him since.

To make matters worse, the asshole had taken most of the cash from her wallet, so I had to send her some money to ensure she could make it back home. I would have taken her myself, but the driver had already arrived.

"That's it. Chill and relax?" Merrick said.

I was caught off guard by his question. It took me a long pause to catch up.

"Yup, that's it. I might do a little shopping, too," I said, attempting to cover my slow response by taking a sip of my wine.

Merrick said nothing, but I could tell he noticed. The man noticed everything. We finished our wine and light conversation before he guided me to a bedroom.

As soon as he opened the door, I was hit with an extreme sense of Deja Vu. This room looked eerily similar to the one at the club – from the bed to the giant mirror and even the ridiculously huge playbox.

The only differences were; this room was bigger, there were no paintings of naked chicks, and the chair that sat against the wall wasn't attached to a chair lift. However, the chair did include straps, gold ones in fact, and I couldn't wait to try them out.

He guided me toward an open area in the room where a thick, brown rope with a round metal clasp at the end hung from the ceiling.

"Take your clothes off," Merrick said.

I laughed.

"Same room, same words," I said.

"What are you talking about?" he asked.

"This room looks identical to the one at the club and the

first thing you said to me in that room was to take my clothes off."

"Oh," he said, understanding dawning. "I had this room designed to look like that one because I liked how well it flowed and clothes are never necessary here."

"That's good news," I said, already tossing my shirt and bra aside.

Once I was completely naked, Merrick bound my wrists.

I stared down at the leather handcuffs. They looked so official. Not at all like the cuffs used by police or the fun ones you see with the pink fuzzy coverings. No, these meant serious business and were made for long-term wear.

Ten links formed a short metal chain connecting the cuffs. The inside of my wrist restraints were lined with a faux fur material that rested tightly, but not uncomfortably, against my skin.

Next, he reached above my head and began pulling on the brown rope. It made a light clicking sound as it stretched lower and lower.

Yanking on the chain of the handcuffs, Merrick used it to lift my hands above my head, but before connecting them to the metal clasp on the rope, he paused.

"Is something on your mind? You've seemed distant ever since you got here."

Shit! Were my emotions still that transparent?

I thought I had put the issues concerning my mom aside. It wasn't like there was anything I could do. She was already back home with a new prescription, so there was no need to worry, but still, I did.

"No sir, I'm fine."

Merrick didn't take his eyes off me. He was waiting for an answer and the one I gave was clearly insufficient.

Giving him a half-truth I said, "It's the cases. I am trying to figure out the best strategy for the company and I tend to get lost in my work."

He connected the clasp of the rope to my cuffs and once he released it, the rope retracted a few inches, forcing me to stand taller.

Merrick tilted my mouth to his and gave me the softest kiss I had ever experienced. I sighed into his mouth, my shoulders relaxing, despite the odd position they were in.

"Don't lie to me," he said.

I licked my lips, still tasting the sweetness of the wine from his kiss.

"Family issues is all."

His eyes softened. "Do you want to talk about it? Or is there anything I can do?"

My answer was honest, "You can fuck me."

"That is going to happen regardless, my dear," he said.

After another quick kiss, Merrick went to grab a long iron bar from his playbox across the room.

Holding it in front of me, he yanked hard.

Not only did I notice the bar double in length, but I'd bet my next orgasm that it also locked in place and he would use it to force my legs to remain spread wide.

"I've seen that before," I said with a sly smile. "What's it called?"

"A spreader bar. And it's good you already know what it is because that means I don't have to explain how it works," he lowered the bar and tapped my inner ankles. "Open up."

I tugged on the rope, but unlike when Merrick pulled on it, the rope didn't drop down lower, which meant I received no slack. It made spreading my legs difficult.

I could feel the stretch all over my body, especially in my back and thighs. My chest arched forward and I stood very still to avoid leaning too far forward or backward.

"This bondage position is sometimes referred to as the

Eiffel tower," he explained, ignoring my balancing act. "Your wrists are tied together and held high above your head, and your legs will be kept apart using this bar."

Merrick fastened one side of the bar to my left ankle, then after adjusting my stance because my legs still weren't wide enough, he connected the other side to my right.

He took a step back and smiled. I imagined I must look like a sexy, nude letter A.

"How does it feel?"

"A little tight, but I'm fine, sir."

"You say that now, but we will see how you feel when I return."

When he what?! My mind screamed.

"You broke the rules when you lied to me," Merrick continued. "And I still owe you for that blatant disrespect in your office before I left. It will do you good to spend some time thinking about what you did."

Oh, he was kidding... he had to be kidding.. he was not kidding.

Merrick began walking towards the bedroom door.

"Wait, when will you come back, sir?" I yelled hurriedly after him.

He opened the door and stopped.

"When I'm ready to fuck you," he said over his shoulder and left.

I hung there, feeling vulnerable and sexually frustrated.

Leaving me like this wanting to be touched, to be used, to be satisfied, was cruel. The ache between my thighs grew and knowing I was powerless to do anything about it made my desire burn to new heights.

I used the time to think about everything and nothing – from the joys and sorrows in my life to how soft his carpet felt under my toes to how cool the room had suddenly become.

Did he turn up the air?

The anticipation of his return was building in me. I was already his for the taking, but this restraint and abandonment brought on desperation. I would do anything for him to let me down from here.

Suddenly, I heard the knob turn and in walked Merrick. *Damn!*

He was naked and very ready. His dick pointed straight out in my direction as if saying, "she is over there let's go get her," and coming to get me, he was.

This punishment would now be over, and I could move on to an evening of pleasurable escape and fulfillment.

I tried to resist asking, but I needed confirmation, "Is my punishment over, sir."

"No, your punishment is far from over."

My eyes dropped to the floor as I tried to hide my disappointment. I wouldn't be getting any action tonight and that was almost maddening.

But then he said, "I have good news for you, though. Tonight you will not be required to ask my permission to cum."

I looked at him quizzically. "I don't... understand, sir?"

It's a fucking trap! My mind screamed.

In one of his hands was a soft, black blindfold.

I don't like this.

The world went dark as he covered my eyes with it and I felt my pulse quicken.

Already I was tied up, subjected to utter loss of control. Restricting my sight as well made me feel boxed in. I had no idea when or *if* he would release me.

Of course, he is going to release you, I rationalized.

I knew with every fiber of my being that Merrick would not hurt me, but this new limitation gave me severe claustrophobic vibes.

Briefly, I contemplated using my safe word, but then I felt

Merrick's hands touching me and it was like a switch flipped. The apprehension eased and my breathing returned to normal. It seemed I didn't need a way out of this. I solely needed to know he was there.

His fingers moved over my chest, down my waist, and along the edges of my pussy. He sank two fingers into me and rotated them at a nice and steady tempo.

In and out... in and out.

My body shook from the sensations. Something strange was happening. It appeared that shutting down one sense magnified the others.

The depths of pleasure, the sounds of his calm and steady breathing, and the fresh scent of the room, now all stood out to me.

"You pushed me that day in your office," I heard him say, "Because you wanted sex."

He twisted his fingers and massaged a delicate spot inside harder.

"And then," he continued. "You came here tonight hoping to escape whatever is on your mind through sex, just like you always do." He picked up momentum. "I guess you weren't lying when you told me you use sex like a pain pill."

My body trembled. I was nearing my peak fast. I fought to keep my balance and hold my position, but I was blindfolded, with my arms stretched above my head and my feet spread so far apart it felt like I was trying to do a split.

Who was I kidding? I was going down.

"Therefore, my slut. I think it's only fitting that tonight I give you as many orgasms as you can handle."

I fell over the edge, hit with a tsunami of explosions. I felt like I was falling, powerless to control my limbs, breathing, or words. My back arched and my toes gripped the carpet as the sound of blood rushing through my body filled my ears.

I didn't know when it happened, but suddenly, I felt like I was floating.

Seconds later, it dawned on me why— I was being carried. Merrick's arm was secured behind my back, the other cradling my knees.

I suppose he had no choice because with my hands still cuffed, legs fixed by the spreader bar, and my eyes covered, there was no way for me to resist or move on my own.

He deposited me onto the bed, and it felt like the room was spinning. Euphoria had me in its grasp, and I didn't want it to let go.

"Are you with me?" Merrick asked.

With the blindfold still on, his voice sounded more intense, or maybe that was just my imagination, sharpened by the darkness and the weight of anticipation hanging in the air.

"Yes... I am."

He lifted my cuffed hands before speaking. "I want you to bend your knees, then hold this bar in place, keeping your legs back and spread for me." After helping me get my hands around the thin metal bar, Merrick said, "Do not let it go, do you understand?"

"Yes, sir."

With a calculated slowness, I felt the softness of Merrick's lips on my inner thighs, working their way over to my pulsating center. When his tongue brushed across my clit, my hands tensed on the bar, fighting the enticement to reach out and grab his head.

I didn't know if I could come again so quickly, but Merrick and his oral talents took care of any doubts. He knew when to go slow and when to move fast, when to suck gently and when to suck hard.

My body was a puppet under his control, and if he wanted another orgasm out of me, he was going to get it.

He flicked his tongue, teased my body, and whispered

filthy things to me for so long that my already weakened legs began to shake again. Then without remorse, his tongue tackled my clit; zeroing in on it, sucking it, pulling it, and rapidly licking me until I begged him to slow down.

My breathing was ragged and although I didn't have asthma, I was starting to believe I wasn't immune from suffering an attack.

I kept trying to squeeze my legs shut, forgetting over and over again that the spreader bar would prevent me from dodging any of this.

It held my legs firmly open, leaving me completely exposed and helpless as Merrick took full control.

Clutching the bar for dear life, my stomach fluttered and the building tension of another release, more untamed than the first, erupted out of me.

I screamed and screamed and screamed, but Merrick gave me no leniency. He ripped my hands from the bar and flipped me over to my stomach.

"Arch your ass up," he commanded, slapping one cheek so hard I cried out.

I tried to push up with my elbows, but my body betrayed me—I slipped back onto the bed. The lingering effects of my second orgasm had left me weak and unsteady.

To make matters worse, being blindfolded with my legs locked into the shape of the letter V didn't leave me with much strength or coordination to obey.

I tried it again and got the same result.

On the third attempt, Merrick helped me. I was grateful for the assistance until I felt him place a small vibrating device on my clit and secured the straps around my waist.

"Wait!" I cried out. "Please, sir, it's too much."

"Not nearly as much as it's about to be," he said, sliding his dick into my pussy.

I sucked in a sharp breath, fisted the sheets with my bound

hands, and clenched my teeth as a new wave of insurmountable pleasure poured in.

No one else but Merrick Alexander would find a vibrator that allowed simultaneous penetration.

He was my antagonist and my hero, propelling me down a dark tunnel that promised treasure, and like a crazy woman, I was along for the ride.

It would be nice if I could catch my breath, though.

My heart was beating so hard I could feel it in my throat. My palms were sweating and I was beginning to feel dizzy.

Merrick suddenly ripped the blindfold from my eyes and grabbed my chin, turning my head to the right.

I blinked several times as my vision adjusted to the light, slowly realizing I was looking at our reflection in a full-length mirror.

"I want you to watch me fuck you," he said. Adjusting his hips to dig into me from a new angle. "And when I am done, I will finish in your mouth."

I wanted to say, "Thank you, sir," because I loved it when he finished in my mouth, especially when he came more than once, giving me massive amounts to swallow, but words were long gone. I was nothing more than a bundle of glorious sensations.

Another climax permeated through me and my body tightened, my vision blurred and my hands ached to be freed.

I needed some semblance of control over this matter, but this man, this Dom, had it all, and he wasn't sharing.

Using the hand not currently gripping my chin, Merrick gathered the chain of my handcuffs and forced me to release the sheets by stretching my arms up toward the headboard.

He held the chain so tight I could no longer grip anything to make this easier.

I stared at our reflection in the mirror, taking in my spread legs, outstretched arms, and Merrick holding my face in place as he moved in and out of me at varying speeds.

The muscles in his arms flexed as he balanced himself with ease while the vibrator hummed with intensity and purpose, stimulating my clit without interruption.

He wanted to punish me and further prove that he owned my body by making me watch and without question, I would let him do it. Surrendering to him gave me a sense of pride that I couldn't explain.

The fourth orgasm rushed in, causing my body to convulse and I didn't even cry out. The sensation was astronomical, but I think all of my moans, sighs, and whimpers were tapped out.

It didn't matter, though, because Merrick didn't stop. He continued hammering into me without regard.

At some point, the overflow of orgasmic ecstasy caused a tear to fall down my cheek. Proving to me just how intense sheer bliss could be.

Merrick gently wiped it away with his thumb and said, "Looks like you are reaching your limits."

The statement reminded me of the reason he gave for wanting to tie me up in the first place.

He'd said he wanted to see what happened when he pushed me past my limits and that if my hands were free, I might try to stop him, and maybe he was right.

This much pleasure could drive someone insane. My body could not continue to take this. It would give out on me, which is probably exactly what happened since everything suddenly went black.

When I regained consciousness, Merrick was sitting next to me, his hand massaging my back. I noticed the cuffs and bar were on the floor next to the bed.

Fogginess clouded my brain. "What happened?" I said.

"You fainted," he replied. "But you were only out for a short while. I've seen this happen before. You are going to be fine."

I wasn't worried, but his reassurance did warm me. He gathered me in his arms and covered me with a blanket.

For the longest time, we lie there in silence while he stroked my hair and caressed my skin.

When he finally helped me sit up, then eventually stand, I instantly missed the security and peace I felt within his arms.

However, I didn't protest. I understood that Merrick's intimate gesture was only his way of checking in to ensure that I felt stable after such a strenuous ordeal. Besides, it was late and I needed to get going anyway.

"Do you need some help getting dressed?" he asked.

I shook my head. Beyond the slight weakness of exhaustion and soreness in my nether region from way too many orgasms, I felt sensational.

Light, elated and unburdened.

Merrick got dressed and left the room. A few minutes after I got dressed and met him in the kitchen. He was stirring a pot of something that smelled heavenly, reminding me I needed to go home and eat.

"Thank you, sir, I had a lovely evening," I said. "I see you are in the middle of setting up your dinner, so I will see myself out."

He stopped stirring the pot and faced me.

"Jocelyn, the only place you are going is to that table to sit down. I made dinner for you."

"I can't believe you cooked for me?!" I said.

I was working on my second bowl of spiced lentil & butternut squash soup. I'd never had this particular soup combination before, and now I would have to look up a recipe. It was fantastic!

Pausing, with my spoon in mid-air, I narrowed my eyes at him, "What's your aim? You've already gotten me into bed."

Merrick sat across from me, a content expression on his face. He finished his meal ten minutes ago after only eating one bowl. Nonetheless, he insisted I have another since I had barely eaten today. It tasted so good I couldn't resist the offer.

"I would have thought you of all people would remember every line of the contract you signed."

When he noticed I wasn't following, he said. "As your dominant, it is my job to take care of your well-being, which includes your safety, mental and emotional health."

I still wasn't buying it. "How is making me dinner taking care of my well-being?"

"Before I left for Miami, I noticed that you often skipped lunch. I can't fuck you if you are always falling out on me," he explained with a straight face.

"So your motivation is entirely self-serving?"

"It is indeed. Like you told me, I'm only here for 'the sex'."

My lips twitched and seconds later, a laugh erupted from me and then from him. He always used my words against me.

"I can't argue with that," I said after our laughter died down. "Where did you learn how to cook?"

"I come from a big family and my parents believed that everyone helps out in the kitchen."

Licking my lips, I dipped my spoon to scoop up another bite.

"Your parents did you a favor. I don't know how to cook much beyond the basics. My dad handled most of the cooking, and I never cared to learn. Now that I'm older, I wish I would have paid more attention."

"I could teach you some things," he said, and then he added with a tease, "That way you wouldn't have to eat so much junk food."

Pointing my spoon at him, yet again to express just how absurd I thought his opinion was, I said, "Excuse you! I will never give up junk food. It's one of my guilty pleasures."

"I can see why. I enjoyed the bag you packed for me. I haven't had candy in a long time."

"That confession is both admirable and terrifying. Did you finish it?"

"I did. I wouldn't make it a habit, but it was a nice change. Thank you."

I gave him a proud smile. "You're welcome."

Sufficiently stuffed, I dropped the spoon and sighed.

"What are your other guilty pleasures?" Merrick asked.

"You," I said without delay.

"Likewise, Ms. Milner," he complimented. "I have been meaning to ask, what do you think about your role as a sub so far? Any major likes or dislikes?"

"I like it all," I said honestly. "I've even learned surprising things about myself."

"Such as?"

"Two things actually. For starters, your dick should be studied because nothing should feel that amazing."

Merrick smiled and said, "I don't know about studied, but I'm glad you're enjoying full use of it."

I fanned myself emphatically and grinned. This man and his words would be the death of me.

"Yes, sir, I am *definitely* enjoying it. The other thing I have learned is that I love rough sex."

"Mmhmm," he said in a deep, low voice. "That is because you are a remarkable woman. The perfect mix of classy and dirty."

"So I've been told," I replied. Since we were on the Dom/sub topic I figured it was the perfect time to bring up something that was on my mind. "Do you mind if I ask you a question?"

Merrick collected the dishes from the table and took them to the sink. I watched him go, a little disappointed that he had put a shirt on.

"Not at all."

"The other day in my office before your trip, was that considered breath play?"

Merrick paused before putting the dishes in the sink. Although he wasn't facing me, I could tell something was wrong by the way his shoulders tensed.

"Yes, it was," he said, lowering the dishes, but he still didn't face me.

I felt the need to fill the silence, so I continued.

"You seemed different somehow that day. I am not complaining," I rushed to add, "because, as I said, I like it rough. I wouldn't even mind if you did it again."

Wouldn't mind, was putting it nicely. I *absolutely* wanted him to do it again.

Merrick finally faced me, nothing in his expression revealing what he was thinking.

He came back to the table and took a seat. "That was a mistake and you won't see that side of me again."

"May I ask why?"

He reached out and touched my face tenderly.

"That, gorgeous, is not up for discussion."

I closed my eyes and relished in his magnetic touch. Evidently, something had happened and it wasn't good. I wanted him to feel comfortable enough to share, but I also understood the need for privacy.

Opening my eyes, I gave him a sincere smile.

"Yes, sir, I understand."

"I will say this, though," his hand dropped from my face, his vibe changing to all Dom and no bullshit. "I have no problems punishing you in the manner that I stated."

"You would really do that?!" I asked, astonished. "Wait! Have you done that?! Chained one of your subs to a wall for an entire weekend?"

"Yes, I have."

"What?!" my eyes widened. I had to repeat the question. Maybe he wasn't understanding. "You chained her to a wall... and forced her to give you oral *all* weekend? She didn't eat anything else!"

I had been doing this sub thing for almost two months and apparently, I still didn't fully comprehend how wild it could get.

"First, I didn't force her to do anything. She could have used her safe word at any time. Second," he added with a chuckle, "I gave her bread and water."

"Wow," I uttered, sitting further back in my seat, amazed and curious.

Merrick shrugged. "She learned her lesson."

"I'll say. What a way to be corrected. I'd love to hear that story from her perspective."

"I can do you one better," he said, "Disrespect me like that again, and you will experience it firsthand."

A wicked smile crossed my lips. "I'll be good, but it does sound kind of hot."

He shook his head.

"You are such a brat."

"A what?"

"A brat. It means that you like to push my buttons or break the rules to get my attention."

"I'm definitely a brat then," I said, committing to the title.

Merrick's phone vibrated and he picked it up. An annoyed expression transformed his handsome face. It likely wasn't any of my business, but seeing him frustrated prompted me to react.

"Is something wrong?" I asked.

He let out a long breath, still studying the phone, his eyes moving rapidly, reading the message.

"I think Shelia is going to be a problem," he said.

"The woman Ashton has a contract with?"

"Yeah."

I remembered meeting Shelia in the break room during my first week there. She was exactly what I expected– beautiful, poised and friendly enough.

However, the reaction she gave when she said she worked for Ashton, was slightly off-putting. The way Shelia clutched her chest and looked far off into the distance made my "there's a psycho within a two-foot radius" alarm go off, but then again, I didn't know her and who was I to judge?

"Why, what happened?" I asked.

Merrick turned the phone off and put it back on the table.

"Doesn't matter," he said. "But since you asked me a question, I would like to ask you one. Why do you avoid romantic relationships?"

I thought about telling him that, like his, this topic was also not up for discussion, but decided against it. That would sound like an eye for an eye and I wasn't that type of woman. Plus, I didn't mind opening up to him. Merrick was a good listener.

"Relationships are a big gamble. You don't always get what you give, and in the rare cases you do, you still seem to come out with the short end of the stick." I couldn't help but think about my mom losing my dad. "Anyway, the way I look at it, trying to find a happily ever after is a risk I'm not interested in taking."

"That's respectable. Have you ever been in a serious relationship?"

"Once, and yes, he did break my heart, cheated on me with my best friend at the time, but I got over it and moved on."

"Or so you thought you got over it," was his ballsy reply.

I gave him a look.

"Why do you say that?"

"Something doesn't add up. I can tell you guard your heart, which I'm not knocking, I'd just like to understand why."

He wasn't wrong, I did guard my heart, but that was the answer he was going to get because sadly, it was the only answer I had. I was no longer sure why relationships were unappealing to me.

For the longest time, I thought I was simply happier without them. The emotions and trust required to have a successful relationship were exhausting and terrifying.

But after being around Merrick, I couldn't help but think, what would it be like to seriously date him? And that question jumpstarted so many more...

Why did I avoid serious relationships? Was it due to the remnants of a broken heart? Watching my mom with Gary? The fear of being rejected? All of the above?

"I'm not some big mystery or puzzle to solve," I said, not

interested in going down this road. "What you see is what you get. But hey! What about you? Have you had your heart broken?"

"Nope. I've never given it to anyone."

Well, well, let's see how he handled being under the spotlight.

"And why is that? Are you afraid of something? Have some big, dark secret?"

"Nothing like that. My interest simply isn't piqued easily, and I've been told I'm a hard man to tame."

"I don't know who said it, but they are right. You will definitely keep a girl on her toes." I smiled at him, a little saddened by my next words. "But keep looking. One day you will find her."

Merrick's response almost stopped my heart.

"I think I already have."

As the months moved along everything work-related and Merrick-related became like second nature.

Meetings... blowjobs... phone calls... orgasms... court-rooms... wild bondage positions... lawsuits, and even more orgasms.

This spontaneous and spicy routine summed up both my position at Dual and my sub-agreement.

We were still very much operating within the confinements of our contract. Although, there were times that Merrick flirted, hinted, or flat out said that he could see this turning into something more.

What that meant exactly, I wasn't sure. I hadn't given into any of those sweet words or subtle, albeit charming actions and didn't plan to. I was convinced that Merrick only wanted me because he couldn't have me, or rather, he couldn't have my heart. Eventually, his fascination would fade, and he'd move on to someone else.

That truth didn't sadden me. I knew what we had was temporary, but currently, my life was good, and I wouldn't change a thing for fear of ruining it.

The same couldn't be said about my mom's life. There was friction between her and Gary, but she never talked about it. During several of my visits to see her, he was passed out drunk on the couch or hadn't come home at all. More late-night gambling shenanigans, no doubt.

I had practically begged her to leave him and move in with me, but she refused, swearing that things were fine and Gary was merely going through a rough patch.

The faint scratches and bruises on her arms and legs suggested there was another story to be told, but in the end, all I could do was take care of her the best I knew how.

She always explained everything away, and I felt like the bad guy pushing her with my opinions and accusations.

I picked up my cup of tea and looked around my office, bringing my mind back to things that brought me joy– law and lust.

Tomorrow I had to make a courtroom appearance to battle several cases. All of them would be pretty much open and closed, but there was one that I would need a continuance for, Dual Construction LLC. vs. Theodore Blakey.

Turns out my suspicions were correct. Theodore was guilty of workers' compensation fraud for conjuring numerous fictional stories about how he got injured and was unable to work.

He'd had some severe injuries from a car accident three years ago. At the time his doctors suggested surgery and for him to avoid high labor jobs, ie, construction work. But Mr. Blakey saw an opportunity to get hired for

Dual and then file claims to get paid for previous injuries.

A very cunning idea, if only he hadn't met me. My thorough investigation into his background revealed his lies and now the truth had him in a chokehold.

I smiled to myself.

It would be nice for Merrick to put me in a chokehold.

I glanced at the clock, it was 8 a.m. In thirty minutes, I would meet Merrick for our occasional morning workout. It was one of our newest and sexiest activities.

Normally, I worked out at home or the local gym a couple of times a week depending on my schedule. But Merrick suggested we do them together.

Inside the building was a private workout room created by (and for) Ashton and Merrick's personal use. The small yet nicely designed gym included state-of-the-art equipment, as well as a shower and steam room.

When our schedules permitted, Merrick and I would work out for an hour, doing various exercises like running, planks, and lifting weights; light ones for me and ridiculously heavy ones for him.

However, no matter what exercise we did last, we always started the workout the exact same way: we would shower together, and then Merrick would do his push-ups.

His very sexy, delicious push-ups.

He normally did one hundred, but due to erotic extenuating circumstances, getting from start to finish sometimes proved challenging.

That was because, to start, I would get completely naked and lie on the mat. Then, with my arms at my side, I positioned myself so that my face lined up with his dick.

He would get into the assumed position with his legs placed widely apart and then begin. Every time he lowered his body, his full length glided easily all the way down my throat.

When he pushed back up, I hungrily sucked on the head, never letting him pull completely free of my mouth and sometimes being rewarded with sweet drops of precum for my efforts.

Merrick's moans of ecstasy were everything to me because they were so sexy and random. He would do several pushups before even a curse or pleasurable sigh escaped his lips.

For a man getting his dick sucked while working out, he had insane concentration. Performing his pushups with ease and precision as he worked his triceps and pectoral muscles to fine-tune his already impressive upper body strength.

With the exception of the occasional compliment such as, "You're such a good, whore" or "You serve your purpose well", he said nothing until he came, usually twice, giving us both an incredible start to our day.

I checked the time again, only five minutes had passed. *Twenty-five more to go.*

I couldn't wait to see him, to touch him, to taste him. Today would be the last day I would spend time with him for five days. He had to catch a flight to Puerto Rico later this morning and wanted to see me before he left.

Dual had won the bid of several major contracts to rebuild areas throughout the island, and it was Merrick's job to oversee the start of these projects.

Wiggling my mouse to wake up my computer, I noticed my phone light up. It was an incoming call from Raquel, a childhood friend. I wondered why she was calling so early then, said a quick prayer that nothing horrible hadn't happened.

"Hi," I said, bracing myself for the worst.

"Hey, Jocelyn! How are you?" Her chipper tone made the tight squeeze in my chest disappear. She didn't sound sad, but she did sound out of breath.

"I'm good. Is everything, okay? You sound like you have been running?"

"That's because I *am* running. I am getting in an early morning workout. They are simply the best!"

"I would have to agree with you there," I said, confident that my reasoning was vastly different from hers.

"I apologize for calling so early, I have been meaning to reach out to you for weeks, but I have been so busy."

"It's no problem, I'm at the office anyway. Do you need something?"

"Nope. I wanted to tell you the good news." There was a brief pause while she caught her breath. Then she said, "Desmond is getting married!"

I sat back in my chair and covered my mouth, an enormous smile spreading across my face. Desmond, or Des, as we called him, was Raquel's younger brother and such a great guy.

"You're kidding! Who's the lucky lady?"

"Her name is Piper and I already love her like a sister." With a laugh, she added, "Get this, her nickname for me is legs."

I thought about Raquel's tall, slim physique. She was a beautiful girl with an equally wonderful heart and always reminded me of someone that belonged on a runway. The name made perfect sense.

"It fits," I said. "You have always had the best legs."

"Thank you, thank you," she said, sounding as if she were on stage about to take a bow. "I'm running to keep these long legs in shape. I can't be looking horrible in my dress."

"Raquel, you couldn't look horrible if you tried."

"Well, I don't plan on trying, which is why I am out here every morning before work."

"Then you will be fabulous forever," I said with a grin.

"I better be!" We shared a laugh and pure joy filled

Raquel's voice. "Oh, Jocelyn, you should see the two of them. Des and Piper are so cute together."

"I'll bet they are. Where will the wedding be?"

"It's six months away and will be held at one of the dreamiest venues I have ever seen off the coast of California. The way I have been running around helping out, you would think I was the bride."

I laughed.

"I know how much you love weddings."

"I'm not the only one," Raquel announced. "When we were teenagers, I recall you having a giant book stuffed with the endless details of your perfect wedding. Whatever happened to that book?"

I still have it, I thought to myself. *In a giant brown box, on the third shelf in my closet, tucked behind the extra bed sheets.*

"Who knows? It's probably somewhere around the house," I said.

"I'd love to see it. Then maybe one day we will be planning your wedding."

I appreciated her enthusiasm.

"I'll let you go first," I said.

"Hey, I'm not going to argue with that," she said with a giggle. "I can't wait to get married one day."

I didn't comment, but Raquel didn't notice because she had started running again. Before Merrick, marriage was an absolute no. But now, my mind was open to all sorts of possibilities.

Although I wasn't trying to get married anytime soon, the idea of a lifetime with someone as mentally and physically stimulating as Merrick didn't seem so scary.

"Anyway," Raquel suddenly said. "I wanted to tell you about the wedding before you got the invitation in the mail. I can't wait to see you."

"Me too! It's been way too long. Maybe we could see each other before the wedding."

"I'd love that! Shoot me some dates that you're free and we will figure it out from there."

"Sounds like a plan."

We ended the call, and I made a note to check my availability. It would be great to see Raquel. The last time I saw her was a couple of years ago and we had a blast.

I didn't see Raquel often because she lived in another state and her schedule was as busy as mine. It was wonderful to hear that she was happy, and I was truly overjoyed for Des. Everyone deserved happiness.

Even those of us that think it isn't possible.

Pushing the melancholy thought away, I focused on a more fond memory, my wedding book. I hadn't thought about it in years and hadn't laid eyes on it for even longer.

It was a thick, black and gold binder stuffed to the max with clippings of wedding dresses, shoes, floral arrangements, color palettes, ribbons, and mock invitations.

I was absolutely obsessed and why wouldn't I be? My wedding had to match the fairytale life I planned to live – married to a rich doctor, with four kids (two boys and two girls), a dog named Bambi and a house in Malibu.

Yep, it was all planned out, but I soon learned that life doesn't care about your plans. What you want isn't always what you get, but what you have can be just as amazing.

And what I had was; a successful career, great friends and genuine peace concerning how my life had turned out. It was okay that things didn't always go as planned because sometimes they did, and in those perfect moments, life was so incredible that it took my breath away.

I looked at the clock. It was time to leave for my workout with Merrick.

Would you look at that? Another perfect moment that would undoubtedly have me gasping for air.

Chapter Eleven

"THE BALLS, TOO?"

I was trembling, weak and couldn't speak. To sum it up, I was overworked and it felt so good.

Merrick had me bent over the back of his desk with my arms stretched up and out. My wrists were tied to the handles of the drawers and my ankles were bound to either side of the desk legs.

Visually speaking, I resembled the letter X, bent at a 90-degree angle and he called this position overworked... merely because it amused him.

To add to the erotic festivities, I was wearing a ball gag. We were in Merrick's office at Dual, and as he so casually reminded me, I'm a screamer. Thanks to this huge plastic ball in my mouth I was also now a drooler, but I didn't give a shit.

What I wanted to do was cum and Merrick wanted to play. No surprise who was winning this battle. I had to wait for him to tell me I was allowed to cum, and so far, nothing.

a, b, c, d, e, f, g....

I was quickly running out of ways to continue holding back. This position allowed for deep penetration and Merrick was hardcore diving into my wetlands.

He had settled into a rhythm that felt so delicious it made my eyes roll to the back of my head. Not to mention, the way he was squeezing my ass while his dick repeatedly slammed into my cervix wasn't helping matters.

"You may be tied down, but you can still move that ass. Roll those hips faster!" he commanded, slapping my ass.

Then came the sensations... the arousing, tingling, warming feeling of his palm connecting to my skin. The pleasure it added to this moment was indescribable. I wanted him to do that again, and seconds later, he did.

The gag prevented me from breathing through my mouth, so I had to be mindful to breathe through my nose. I Inhaled deeply, Merrick's woody and spicy scent filling my nostrils and driving the eroticism of this act to new extremes.

Peter Piper picked a peck of pickled peppers.

Nope, thinking about tongue twisters wouldn't work either. In this case, Merrick was my Peter and his pickle was pecking the hell out of me.

Merrick relocated one of his hands from my ass and placed it over my pussy. Isolating my clit with his thumb and forefinger, he kneaded and massaged it in a circular motion, and I was propelled into sensation overload.

I squeaked, my back arching, lifting me only a few inches before the restraints tugged me down again.

My eyes found the wood grain pattern on Merrick's desk. With my cheek resting against the smooth, sleek surface, this up-close view made the design look like a million squiggly lines huddled close together. I would simply count those lines to keep my mind occupied.

1, 2, 3, 4, 5... just cum already! I mentally yelled at him.

Of course, he didn't, and I was forced to endure more of his ravishing torture. Eventually, while pounding himself to new lengths inside me, he asked, "Are you ready to cum?"

Did people need air to breathe? Did fish swim? Was I so wet that I was possibly dripping all over his floor?

I nodded frantically.

"I need you to agree to something first."

I moaned, ready to agree to anything he wanted and nodded again.

"Let me take you on a date."

My heart skipped a beat.

He wanted a date. An actual date.

Up until this point, the only times Merrick had taken me out to dinner were related to work. This would be something different, it would be romantic, and I didn't have the strength to rationalize the reasons why it wouldn't be a good idea.

Then, being the oh-so-cruel, unbelievably skilled lover he was, Merrick leaned forward and stretched his body out over mine. His hands slid down my arms, intertwining his fingers with mine, his chest pressed firmly against my back and his deepening stroke manipulated the answer right out of me.

I moaned again, louder this time and bobbed my head in agreement.

"Good girl," he said into my ear. "You may cum."

And cum I did. My legs gave out and my pussy clenched so hard around him I felt it in my stomach, back and chest. My muffled cries leaked out from behind the gag, barely louder than a whisper.

Merrick came seconds after me and I vaguely realized that he always let me cum first, unless I was being punished, and that was so sexy.

"Asking me out on a date when I was in such a vulnerable position was a low blow," I said after I was dressed and cleaned up.

"I had to be sure you'd say yes," was his unapologetic reply.

It was only 11 a.m. and now that we'd had some fun it was

time for business. We were both preparing to leave his office; Merrick for a meeting in the conference room, and me to check emails.

I shook my head. I would never admit it to him, but I was looking forward to this.

"So what day should I be ready? Friday? Saturday?"

Merrick picked up his suit jacket.

"No, I'll let you know. It likely won't be this week or the next. I have a few things to handle first."

I placed a hand on my hip, feeling slight soreness in my arm thanks to his rope tricks.

"Seriously, Merrick?! You ask me on a date and now you're going to make me wait?"

He stopped gathering his stuff and smiled at me.

"Good things come to those who wait. I just proved that to you," he said, nodding at the desk I was recently strapped down to.

"Ha ha, you're so funny," I said, unamused. "I have to get back to work."

"Yes, you do. I want to see a summary of all the quarter-end cases by noon tomorrow."

"You'll have it by the end of business today," I said over my shoulder on my way out the door.

My inbox was flooded with emails. I'd checked it before I left for Merrick's office an hour ago, but things stayed busy here.

My desk line rang and I answered.

"Jocelyn Milner speaking."

"Ms. Milner, this is Richard Joles attorney for Boulder Parts, do you have a moment to talk?"

Here we go, I thought.

Boulder had been a pain in my ass since this case began four months ago. The construction tools we rented from them kept having to be replaced because a chip inside was faulty and that resulted in hundreds of lost hours toward construction deadlines.

It turned out that the model Boulder rented out to Dual never passed inspection.

"Yes, Mr. Joles. I have time. How may I help you?"

"My client wants a new deal," he said, cutting to the chase.

I sat back in my chair and crossed my legs.

"Your client has no room to make demands."

"Ms. Milner, Boulder is not at fault here. That equipment passed inspection, we have the paperwork to prove it. Dual can not hold us accountable."

I lived for this.

"I am glad that you have the paperwork, it is going to be beneficial for you whenever Boulder files their lawsuit against the company that falsified documents and told them that their defective equipment had passed inspection. But that, Mr. Joles," I said with an unwavering tone, "is not Dual's problem. Boulder is responsible for taking care of the damages that we suffered. We are not concerned with how it happened or why. All we want is for you to stop giving us excuses and start giving us reasonable offers."

There was a long pause then Richard said, "You are asking for forty percent over the total cost. My client will only give you ten."

Ten percent didn't begin to scratch the surface of what we wanted. Dual would be satisfied if I got twenty-five percent. I was pushing for the extra fifteen to give us room to negotiate, but until Boulder came close to at least the twenty-five percent Dual wanted, there would be no deals.

"Mr. Joles, with all due respect, if this case requires an arraignment, not only will we press for the full forty percent, but we will also demand full coverage of legal fees and bill you for time wasted. Do not force our hand because if you do, we will prosecute your client to the fullest extent of the law."

"I will speak to my client, but I suggest you do the same. Forty percent is not a fair number."

"Look at that! I just spoke to them. They want the whole thing," I responded sarcastically.

"I'll be in touch," he snapped, hanging up on me.

He knew he'd have to do better than that. I couldn't care less about his reactions. I only wanted results.

The next few hours were as hectic as my call with Richard. By the time 2 o'clock rolled around, I needed a drink and lunch.

My desk line buzzed. Thankfully it wasn't another lawyer, only Amber.

"Yes."

"Someone is here to see you," Amber said.

"I'll be right there."

I wasn't expecting anyone, so I had no idea who it could be. When I rounded the corner, I found Jada standing there. I walked a little faster, excited to see her.

"Hi, Jada!" I said, hugging her. "What a pleasant surprise."

"I thought so. I was in the area and decided to stop by for lunch. Please tell me you are still a slacker about eating on schedule and haven't had lunch?"

Her look was hopeful.

"I'm still the slacker you know and love," I said.

We laughed and I think Amber rolled her eyes. I turned, about to lead Jada toward my office, when something interesting happened.

Merrick and Ashton were approaching, and it was like watching one of those slow-motion scenes you see in movies. Jada, Amber, and I froze to watch the eye candies scroll by.

Both men were dressed in their usual business attire, tailor-fitted suits. They definitely looked more like male models than they did business owners.

Then again, maybe I was biased since the last CEO I

worked for was in his mid 60's, grumpy and shaped like a Pillsbury dough boy.

"Ladies," Merrick said as they passed by us.

Ashton nodded his hello and gave us all a knee-weakening smile. The effect didn't last as long on me because my eyes darted back to Merrick and my mind wandered off to our hot and heavy encounter from this morning.

However, I think Jada got several degrees warmer staring at Ashton because she wiped her forehead and cleared her throat.

And Amber was like a puppy yearning for attention.

"If you need anything, Mr. Kent or Mr. Alexander, please let me know."

She sounded so desperate I wanted to slap her. I turned around and gave her a cold stare. Ashton and Merrick were now out of earshot.

"What?" she snarled at me, her voice and vibe back to its usual bitchness.

"I hope someone puts you on a leash and leaves your thirsty ass near a fire hydrant," I said and grabbed Jada's arm, pulling her toward my office.

"What the hell is that supposed to mean?" Amber called out behind me.

I ignored her.

We made it back to my office, where I spent ten minutes, per Jada's request, telling her about my morning delight with Merrick.

"What do you want to eat?" I asked, searching the internet for local restaurants that delivered.

"Whatever is okay with me," Jada said. She leaned closer over my desk. "I can see it now."

I scanned the list of available food choices. "See what?"

"Why you sold the rights to your pussy to that gorgeous

man. The company picture you showed me of him did not do him justice. I'll bet he has women falling at his feet."

A laugh burst from me.

"I did not sell my rights.... okay, well, maybe I did, but in my defense, Merrick takes *very* good care of it."

"I can tell. You have been glowing since you began working here, and I saw how you watched him. He owns your ass."

"I am surprised you could see anything with the way your eyes were glued to Ashton."

"What?!... I did... he was... you..."

"Save it! You can't even find the words."

"Was I that obvious?" Jada asked, embarrassed.

"Is water wet?"

Jada made an exasperated sound and covered her face.

"I can't believe I was so obvious!"

"Well, believe it because you were, but I am sure Ashton appreciated the unspoken compliment," I teased.

Jada groaned louder. She was mortified.

"Hey, it's alright. I'm sure Ashton is used to it. I wish he was available because I would set you up with him."

"Don't you dare!" she said, cutting her eyes at me. "Even if he was available, I wouldn't know what to do with that man. Did you see those hazel eyes?! They practically glowed and he looks intimidating as hell. As a matter of fact, they both do. I can see why they are friends."

"That's what I said!" I exclaimed.

We settled on having chicken salad delivered from a nearby cafe. Jada loved salads. I tolerated them, but I preferred steaks, burgers and pasta.

We ate lunch, for the most part, in comfortable silence, which was something I loved about our friendship. We didn't always need to talk to bond. Her presence was enough for me.

"What's the deal with Amber?" Jada asked, opening another pack of salad dressing.

"Other than the fact that she is going to make me stab her with a letter opener, I'm not sure. She has been a bitch since the first day I met her."

Jada narrowed her eyes at me. "Is that all there is to it?"

"Yup, I don't like Amber or the way she stares at Merrick."

Jada gasped. "You have never been territorial over a guy before. You like him!"

"I do not."

"Yes, you do," she insisted. "You've fucked around so much you've finally found a guy that fucked some sense into you. I knew you were playing a dangerous game with this one."

"Again, there is nothing between us, and the only game I am playing is the one where I try to fit Merrick's pool stick and balls into my lady pocket."

"The balls too?!" Jada exclaimed, trying to maintain a straight face.

"If they'll fit," I said with a snicker.

"You're so bad. I love it!"

"Good because all I care about is the sex."

Jada commented, possibly to disagree with me, but I didn't hear her because my attention turned to my cell vibrating across my desk.

I picked it up and studied the unfamiliar number displayed on my screen. Holding up a finger to Jada, I answered the call.

"Hello."

"Hi, is this Jocelyn Milner?"

"It is."

"My Name is Maria and I am calling from Mountain View General Hospital. You are listed as an emergency contact for Joann Milner. It seems she has had a terrible fall and..."

No, no, no, no, no.

I zoned out and the phone slipped from my hand. I scrambled to pick it up, trying to calm my racing thoughts enough to comprehend what the woman was saying.

"Elevated blood pressure... broken arm... come down right away."

My mind wasn't deciphering the message properly. Only assaulting me with bits and pieces that had me grabbing my keys and moving toward the door without realizing it.

I couldn't concentrate. I couldn't focus. I couldn't breathe. My mom was hurt.

Some way, somehow. I made my way out of the office with the vague recollection of Jada offering to drive me to the hospital, but I declined. I had to get to her, I had to see her, and if that shit stain Gary hurt my mom, I was going to lose it.

There was no way the woman sleeping in the large hospital bed was my mom. She was so small. Smaller than the last time I saw her.

Is that even possible?

She was only five feet and weighed around 110 pounds, but this woman, the woman that lay before me, was definitely under 100 pounds. Her left arm was in a cast, bound and resting across her stomach above the white bed sheets. Her face didn't hold an expression of pain, which was good.

The nurse informed me they would be keeping her for a few days due to the hypertensive urgency.

Apparently, when she arrived in the ambulance, not only was her arm broken, but she was complaining of back pain and her blood pressure was 180/120. Shortly thereafter it had risen even higher.

I prayed that her kidney disease wasn't worsening. I helped her keep a close watch on it and she had been in the early stages for years. If the disease had advanced my mom would need to start dialysis and I couldn't imagine the blow that would have on her.

How long would it be before we had more results? Why weren't the blood pressure meds working thus far?

My steps were muted as I forced myself to move further into the room. I didn't want to be in here silent, waiting to ask more questions.

I wanted to be screaming, moving mountains to keep her safe, and getting answers.

Her eyes were closed. Therefore, I lowered myself into the empty chair next to her bed. I wanted to reach out and touch her hand, lay a gentle kiss on her cheek, but she was resting and I didn't want to wake her.

However, a moment later, I watched her eyes flutter open. She looked around, seemingly dazed, then focused on me.

"Jocelyn, what are you doing here?" she asked, her voice frail and surprised.

I bent down to kiss her cheek and closed my hand around hers.

"Mom, I am your emergency contact. You know if they call I will always drop everything and be by your side."

She sighed and closed her eyes, keeping them closed for a lot longer than I think she intended.

"I told the doctor not to call you. That you are an important lawyer who doesn't need to be disturbed with nonsense."

"Nonsense?" I said, adjusting my stance so that she could better see my face. "I spoke to the nurses."

Her eyes closed again, but this time her lips straightened into a defiant line.

"They are making it out to be worse than it is, Jocelyn."

"Okay," I said carefully. "Tell me what happened to your arm?"

"I fell stepping down off the front porch."

With her uninjured hand, she reached down and twiddled with imaginary lint on the white blanket and my blood boiled. Even without my finely tuned lawyer instincts, I could tell she was lying.

I chose my next words carefully, "Was Gary around?"

She was quiet for way too long before saying, "He was. I think he had come outside to get something from his truck."

I am going to kill that bastard.

Tabling the questions about Gary for now, since I knew it would be a dead end, I said, "Do you know what's happening with your blood pressure? Have you not been taking your meds?"

"I have... but sometimes I forget with everything going on... it easily slips my mind."

'Everything going on' meant we were back to Gary.

"You can't spend all your time worrying about Gary, mom."

"He is going through a rough patch and he needs help, Jocelyn. It can't always be about me."

"Dammit, Mom!" I said harsher than I meant. "It's never about you. It's always about him. You have to take care of yourself."

"I do take care of myself. Forgetting isn't a crime, you are just upset for no reason. I know you don't like Gary, but you shouldn't blame him."

"I shouldn't blame him! Why not? He hits you, don't think I haven't noticed the bruises. And he is the reason your arm is broken and your illness is worsening. He lies to you and he uses you. He is damn well to blame."

"You are overreacting," she said, still in denial.

"Mom, what if he kills you one day? You are so fragile and your body can't handle -"

"Stop it! Jocelyn. I am going to be okay. Gary is not a danger to me. Yes, he has faults, but he and I can work through this. You can't just run away every time things get hard. Everyone isn't like you."

Her eyes darted up to mine, apologetic as soon as the words left her mouth.

"What do you mean, like me?"

She sighed.

"I don't remember the last time you were in a serious relationship. When your father died, I should have given you more love... more time... more something. I think you are afraid to trust and maybe somehow that's my fault."

"It's not your fault," I said, hating that she was blaming herself. "I don't need a relationship to be whole. There is no reason for me to seek that."

"Sweetie, it's one thing not to seek out a relationship, but to work so hard actively avoiding them is another. We all need someone and even though Gary is flawed, he is my someone."

I couldn't believe what I was hearing. *Was she going to stay with him? Even after this? I refused to allow it to happen.*

"You deserve better than that. After they release you from here, come home with me? I can take care of you. You won't have to worry about anything."

She gripped my hand. The look in her eyes gave me the heartbreaking response that words could not. She wouldn't leave him.

"Mom, please," I begged, tears falling down my face. "I can't lose you too. You are all I have left."

She touched my face, wiping the tears away.

"I love you very much. You are beautiful, strong, courageous, and successful. You have made me and your father so proud. Promise me you will never forget that."

My heart was broken.

Maybe I wasn't going to lose her today, but I would lose her someday, and whether it be to the illness or at Gary's hand, I was powerless to stop it.

Chapter Twelve

"SO YOU WANT TO BE PUNISHED?"

I weaved in and out of traffic, rushing to my mom's house. What would I do when I got there? I didn't know, but I was furious and Gary had to be confronted.

It wasn't the smartest idea and definitely not the safest, but the fury I felt needed an outlet. I barely remembered the drive over, jumping out of my car, or opening my mom's front door to tear my way through an empty house.

My guardian angel must have been watching over me because the hour I spent sitting in her driveway, waiting for Gary, actually calmed me down.

However, the trouble with letting go of anger is that it made room for other emotions to take over and I wasn't ready.

Devastation, sorrow, grief and helplessness broke down my walls and engulfed me.

I didn't like this. I was afraid and I couldn't handle being alone. That actualization terrified me even more. Normally I preferred isolation in my most vulnerable times.

I was supposed to hold up others, not the other way around, and accepting that I needed someone at my lowest point broke me.

I called Jada, but it was after midnight and she didn't answer. I could have gone to her house anyway, woken her up, and she would have welcomed me with open arms.

Instead, I let my emotions lead and that was how I ended up at Merrick's door.

I rang the doorbell, not considering until after I pressed it that he might not have even been home. It was now close to one in the morning and sheer panic flooded me.

What was I doing here? What would I say? What would he say? This is so stupid. I am crossing a major line. No wonder he didn't allow his subs to know where he lived.

The only time I was expected to come to Merrick's house was when he invited me. He had not invited me. Yet, here I was unannounced, at a ridiculous hour, to do what? Share my fucking feelings?

I was crossing a line and I had to get out of here fast, but of course, before I could run the door opened, and there he stood. Immediately I recognized the questions and confusion etched on his face and knew I'd made a grave mistake.

Before he could say anything, I lifted my hands in apology. "I'm so sorry."

I hurried toward my car, hearing him call my name, but I kept walking, embarrassment carving its way onto my already long list of emotions.

His hand gripped my shoulder and I faced him, fighting back the tears and hurt that would betray my words.

"I'm fine, Merrick. Please, go back inside. I apologize for disturbing you."

This was a hell of a time to request that he leave me alone, but it was all I could do. I really wished I could take these last several minutes back.

What was I thinking coming here?

"What's wrong, Jocelyn?" Merrick said, watching me intently.

He was level-headed and direct, as always. It was me who was losing it.

"I need to go home, that's all."

"Come inside."

I shook my head and backed away. "No, thank you. I'd really rather not."

"It's not a question," he said.

For the first time that night, I looked into his eyes. I wasn't going to talk my way out of this.

I reluctantly followed Merrick into his house. He offered me a drink, but I declined. I wouldn't be staying long.

He sat down on the couch and I remained near the door, probably looking like a mess.

"Why are you standing?" he asked.

I squared my shoulders and said, "Because I'm about to leave."

Merrick sighed as if he were trying to ensure his patience remained intact.

"You are not about to leave," he responded coolly. "You are going to tell me what is going on. What happened when you left work today? Your friend told me it was something about your mom."

Shit!

I had completely forgotten about my sudden departure and abandoning Jada in my office. I stared straight ahead at the wall, feeling mine build back up. I was so tired.

"I already told you, Merrick, nothing is going on," I said flatly.

"Jocelyn," he said disapprovingly, "are you lying to me?"

That's when it dawned on me. The reason I'd come here wasn't accidental or impulsive—it was deliberate. I was running.

Running from the noise in my head, from the ache in my chest that refused to quiet down, no matter how hard I tried to ignore it. Merrick was an escape, plain and simple. With him, I didn't have to think or hold myself together.

He could punish me, push me, and strip me down to

something raw and uncomplicated. With him, there were no expectations beyond the moment.

Only sensations, control, release. And right then, that felt like the only kind of relief I knew how to reach for.

I straightened and locked eyes with him. "Yes, sir, I am lying to you," I confessed.

I thought he would stand, approach me, bring out the rope... something, but he didn't move.

"Why?" he asked.

"Why what?" I snapped, annoyance filling in where my hurt was.

Either he was letting my insolent tone slide or he didn't notice it because, in a calm steady voice, he said, "Why are you lying to me, Jocelyn? What's wrong?"

"NOTHING IS WRONG!" I screamed. "Stop asking me questions and fuck me! Isn't that what you are supposed to do?"

"Jocelyn," he said in warning, but I ignored it.

I was unhinged and on a roll, fueled by recklessness and a need to feel something, anything, other than this hollow ache.

Maybe if I pushed hard enough, he'd finally snap, lose control, and stop holding back.

So I leaned into it, pressing every button I knew, daring him to respond and take advantage of me.

"Isn't that the whole reason I signed the agreement?" I continued. "I don't want to talk. I want to fuck. Why in the hell don't you understand that?!"

I shouted more things that were rude, spiteful and inconceivable, disregarding every warning and order he gave until...

"ENOUGH!" Merrick shouted, rising from the couch.

The sudden boom of his commanding voice silenced me, but not my pain. Tears sprang forth and streamed down my face.

Merrick stepped closer, but instead of seeing his face, I saw his feet because I was staring at the floor. I couldn't bare to glimpse the pity and disgust I knew had to be present in his eyes.

"So you want to be punished?" Merrick asked, his voice low and measured.

The question hung heavy in the air, waiting for an answer I couldn't give. I didn't trust my voice, didn't trust myself. So I said nothing.

I stood there, motionless, staring at the floor as the tears continued to fall, splashing softly against the wood.

When he spoke again, his voice was decisive and unyielding. "Then, I will punish you." My breath hitched at the finality in his tone. "Go upstairs," he continued, "to the first room on the right and get undressed."

I climbed the stairs slowly, following his instructions. I opened the door, so lost in the disturbing thoughts replaying in my head that I barely noticed my surroundings.

"Stop asking me questions and fuck me! Isn't that what you are supposed to do?"

I winced as I recalled my harsh words. It was not only disrespectful to him as my Dom, it was rude in general. Merrick did not deserve my anger. All he did was try to offer me a listening ear after I had invaded his private time, and I used him as a verbal punching bag.

I removed my clothes, wondering what he would do to me. Truth be told, I didn't care. I was safe with him and I trusted him, that was good enough for me.

The creek of the door signaled that Merrick had arrived. I was naked and waiting for his instructions. When I felt his presence behind me, I didn't move. I was just glad he was there.

What he did next was odd, but again... whatever, I had no complaints. I was still trying to hold myself together.

Gathering up my hair, Merrick tied it into a ponytail.

He repositioned himself in front of me and I refused to look up. My goal was to avoid his eyes, but he didn't allow it. Cupping my face in one of his large hands, I was forced to meet his gaze.

He traced the bottom of my lip with the edge of his thumb and said, "You've taken off your clothes. Now, I want you to take off your armor."

And that broke me.

Whatever fragile walls I had left crumbled entirely. I'd fought so hard to stay strong, to keep it all together, but I couldn't anymore.

My heart was in too much pain, causing the tears I'd been holding back to finally spill free.

Instead of being disgusted or annoyed, Merrick leaned down and kissed me passionately and oh so softly.

It felt as if everything I'd been keeping inside was pouring out of me: the fear, the exhaustion, the ache of being lost for so long.

The tears came faster.

Quiet at first, then uncontrollable. I couldn't stop them even if I wanted to.

As quickly as they surfaced and fell, Merrick wiped them away with his thumb, reverent and patient, as though my tears were something precious rather than something to be ashamed of.

He took my hand, leading me into a huge bathroom that resembled a luxurious spa and turned on the shower. I would have spent more time appreciating how upscale, glossy and extravagant everything was, but my heart wasn't in it.

I felt broken, but after what Merrick had said to me, I also felt seen, understood, and cared for. I could release the hurt, and even if just for tonight, I was free to fall apart.

No strength required, no battles to fight, and no debates to win.

I could simply breathe and that made me cry even more as he guided me into the oversized glass square.

Powerful jets of warm, soothing water sprayed me from every angle and it felt divine.

Lathering up a washcloth, Merrick pulled me close and started washing my body. The man washed every inch of me and as the tears fell the shower rinsed them away. Even though I couldn't see them, I imagined they were going down the drain.

After drying me off he carried me to the bed where he proceeded to give me a massage. If it weren't for my damn broken heart I would have been in paradise.

Merrick knew what I needed before I did. He worked his hands all over my body, melting the tension away.

Words were of no use, he communicated with me through touch and I knew then that everything would work out.

In his arms, naked and all cried out, I felt depleted of energy.

The only thing left for me to do was to rest, which I did as I drifted off to sleep.

The next morning, I woke to the smell of pancakes. I rolled over and noticed Merrick had left a nice little care package on the nightstand; one of his shirts, a toothbrush and a note:

Come downstairs when you're ready.

I dropped the note back on the nightstand and closed my eyes. I was an absolute shitstorm last night. With all the blubbering I did, I'm surprised it wasn't a goodbye letter that read...

You drowned me in your tears. Catch you in the next life.

Sighing, I collected my things and went to the bathroom to clean myself up. Even though there was some residual gloom left over from yesterday, I did feel a million times better.

Later I would call and check on my mom, right now, it was time to face Merrick.

"Hi," I said quietly, entering the kitchen.

Merrick's smile warmed me. It was natural with no trace of judgment, disgust, or irritation.

"Hi, beautiful. That shirt looks good on you."

I glanced down at the shirt. It was comfortable, dark blue and stopped just above my knee.

"How do you feel?" he asked.

"Amazing… thanks to you," I added, feeling the embarrassment even though he'd made it clear I had no reason to be. "Do you need me to do anything?"

"No, I'm finishing up now. Take a seat and I will bring you your plate."

I did as told, his long shirt rising up my legs as I sat.

Merrick brought over my food and my stomach danced for joy. My last meal was a salad with Jada yesterday so I was long overdue for food.

Note to self, don't forget to call Jada.

That's when I also remembered that it was Friday and I should be at work.

I covered my face with my hands and groaned.

"What's wrong?" Merrick asked.

"I'm supposed to be at work today."

"Don't worry, I'm giving you the day off."

"I appreciate that, but I have meetings, emails and—"

"All of which you can do from here," he said. "I have a home office remember? Stop finding excuses to get out of this. We need to talk."

Merrick pulled out a chair for himself and sat down. He was wearing my favorite, jeans and a t-shirt. I loved how the shirt hugged his muscles and hung low on his hips.

It made him look down to earth, boyish and inviting, while his suits gave him a sophisticated, cutthroat business edge that warned lines should not be crossed.

"Where's your food?" I asked.

"I already ate," he replied.

"Oh," was all I said.

Picking up the syrup, I poured some on my pancakes. The thick liquid drizzled down the side and made its way over to my eggs. Merrick was waiting for me to speak, and I had no idea where to begin, so I went for a light-hearted icebreaker.

"That was a hell of a punishment last night," I said jokingly.

"And it was exactly what you deserved," he replied.

I gave him a quizzical look. The shower and massage were helpful and possibly needed, but deserved? What game was he playing?

"I deserved a relaxing shower and a sensual massage?" I asked.

"Not being allowed to escape your emotions is what you deserved. You wanted sex so that you could bury your emotions and I wanted you to face them."

I made a sound that fell between a laugh and a sob.

"In that case," I said. "You won. With all the crying I did I definitely faced them. Every bit of last night is crystal clear."

Every single minute, I thought to myself once again, reliving the humiliation.

"Good. That's a start," Merrick announced. "Maybe now

you will remember that my dick is for enjoyment purposes only. All real problems should be directed toward me."

I laughed, thankful for his comedic relief.

"There's that smile I like to see," he said. Then with sincerity in his voice, he asked, "How's your mom?"

I stiffened. It was time to share. Picking up a forkful of eggs, I chewed, swallowed, took a few seconds to appreciate how flavorful it was, then dived into the conversation.

"She's okay. She has a broken arm and they are keeping her due to high blood pressure and back pain. My mom has kidney disease so those symptoms are possible red flags."

"I'm so sorry," Merrick said with genuine concern. "Is there anything I can do?"

I shook my head. "No, I am waiting on a full report from the doctor."

"Do you expect that today?"

"I'm not sure," I said. "But we shall see. Later I plan to go check on her."

"Take all the time you need," he offered. "I understand how stressful it is when someone you care about is hurting."

I quickly debated how much more I wanted to say. I could leave it there and not mention the deeper reasons I was torn to shreds last night, but he deserved the truth, and I think I needed to talk about it.

"That's not the only reason I was sad yesterday," I added quietly.

Merrick didn't say anything, giving me the time and space to gather my words.

"The reason my mom broke her arm was because of my stepdad. I don't know what exactly he did because she wouldn't tell me, but I know he hits her."

"Are you fucking serious?!" Merrick said. "Please tell me she is going to press charges?"

His reaction stunned me. I expected sympathy, not empathy. Instead of the general pity I anticipated, Merrick appeared to understand exactly how I felt. Like it was someone he cared about being abused, and he wanted to go bash Gary's head in right along with me.

Was this hitting close to home for him? Or, and this was a giant leap on my part, did he care more about me than I gave him credit for?

Either way, his reaction made my heart smile even while the reality reinforced the melancholy.

I shook my head.

"She has been with Gary for over ten years, and this isn't the first incident. I've tried to get her to leave, God knows I have, but it's useless. After last night, I truly realized that she isn't going anywhere."

"Is she afraid of him?" Merrick asked, trying to understand.

"No, I think it's more of some twisted obligation to him or possibly a fear of the unknown."

Merrick nodded, then asked, "Do you think she also feels leaving him might be a burden on you? You know, because you will have to care for her physically and financially?"

I gave a pitiful laugh.

"Definitely not, I already do that. Gary doesn't do shit. I handle all of her appointments, medications, and pay all the bills. If anything, it would lessen my burden if I only had to provide shelter for her and not her abuser as well."

That last part I didn't mean to say. I simply got too caught up in venting my frustrations.

Merrick sat back in his chair and wiped a hand over his face.

"Why didn't you talk to me?" he finally said.

I stared at him dumbfounded. He had to have known the answer to that.

"Because it's not your problem!" I stressed. "You are my Dom, not my therapist. You don't have time for all that."

"I would have made time," he responded.

I opened my mouth, trying to find the proper words to get him to understand how crazy that was.

"But... you can't... we don't..." He crossed his arms as if nothing I could say would justify me not shoveling my problems onto his plate. I finally found my voice. "Merrick, this isn't part of our agreement."

"Why not?" he challenged.

I threw up my hands, exasperated. He had to be joking. Surely he understood why I shouldn't come to him with my issues.

"Our agreement is sex! Not for me to run to you every time life gets hard, which by the way," I said, trying to regain some dignity, "contrary to last night, running to people with my problems is not what I do."

"Maybe it's time you start," he offered.

I rolled my eyes. "It's not that easy. I'm used to depending on myself, and I am a private person."

"Oh, I've noticed," he said. "And I am telling you I don't care."

I gave up and began eating my food, going through the motions more than actually tasting anything. It was easier to focus on something small and tangible than to keep fighting a losing battle.

Pouring my heart and soul out had never been who I was anyway. I wasn't built for emotional confessions.

So I chewed and swallowed, retreating inward once more, trying to let the conversation die rather than exposing any more of myself than I already had.

For a few minutes, I thought it would work, but then Merrick asked, "Do you know what submit means?" and I somehow knew he hadn't dropped anything. He was merely approaching it from a different angle.

I sighed. "Yes, Merrick, I know what submit means."

"You don't act like it," was his response. "I don't only expect you to give me your body, I expect you to give me your problems. If something is too heavy for you to carry, come to me, and I will carry it for you."

I dropped my fork. Why couldn't he be happy with just sex? Last night was nice, magical even, but that wouldn't last. He would grow tired of being there for me and it would destroy what we did have. That's why I had to stop this. Sharing time was over.

"What do you want from me, Merrick?" I asked, my voice laced with the weariness I felt. "Last night was a one-time thing. I can't, and I won't add my hardships to your life."

"You can and you will," he said, unmoved.

I blew out a breath and narrowed my eyes. "And what will you do if I refuse? You can't make me come to you."

Merrick gave me his signature "gotcha now" smile. It meant he'd devised an evil plan and I was about to be his test subject.

"You're right I can't." he said. "Therefore, I won't make you cum at all."

Shit!

Chapter Thirteen

It had been three weeks.

Three weeks of no sex, no elaborate bondage positions and no orgasms... at least not for me. Merrick had orgasms every day, sometimes twice a day, thanks to all the blowjobs I was required to give him, and although I loved servicing his needs, it made the denial of my own that much worse.

It wasn't that I couldn't go without sex. I had often gone long periods without it, but that was before I met Merrick, and not having sex with him was a different ballgame.

It wasn't just the physical satisfaction I missed, it was the mental and spiritual connection I craved. The chemistry we shared pushed our intimacy to new bounds and my body longed for the release only he could provide.

After our talk that morning, he'd decided that denying me sex would teach me a lesson about respect and force me to find a new outlet when things got difficult in my life.

Internally I rolled my eyes at that, but aloud I only said, "I'll do my best, sir."

I had learned two things about punishments from Merrick; they always left me wanting him and he was very stern about them. I never knew when they would end or how uncomfortable they would be, and I wasn't allowed to ask.

So I accepted this current punishment with the subservient and grateful attitude he expected while hoping it would be over soon.

However, being the generous Dom he was, his words, not mine, I could earn my way back to his bed. All I had to do was open up to him.

That earned him another one of my infamous eye rolls, but again, I complied.

I'd talked about everything—my mom, my dad, my childhood as a whole, my hobbies, my career, even the reason I'd chosen *red rose* as my safe word.

Coincidentally, red roses were tied to the very reason I'd developed such a deep distaste for Gary.

The first time he hit my mom, he was expectedly apologetic, claiming to be heartbroken and promising that it would never happen again. Regardless of his pleadings, my mom refused to take him back, then one day, he sent her a red rose.

The next day, he sent another and this display of affection went on for two weeks.

Every day I watched her wear down until eventually, she succumbed to his counterfeit charms. Her acceptance of his abuse never made any sense to me because my father wasn't a violent man, but in the end, she forgave Gary again and again.

For some reason, I never forgot the rose ordeal. Possibly because, at one point and time, red roses were my favorite. They matched the fairytale in my head on a long list of romantic gestures the man I eventually loved would do for me.

It plagued me that Gary could take something so lovely and use it to manipulate his way back into my mom's heart. Anyway, from then on, red roses lost their beauty and purity to me.

I always hoped that one day someone special would be able to help restore my love for the sweetly scented flowers, but that never happened.

Everything I told Merrick flowed naturally. I don't know what it meant for him, but for me, it had nothing to do with contracts, orders from my Dom, or me trying to have sex with him again. It was simply time I shared.

Merrick was a good listener and he often offered kind words and advice. I hated to admit it to myself, but despite my initial resistance, it felt therapeutic to share... so share I did.

From my perspective, I'd dug deep, but it appeared Merrick didn't share the same sentiments because here I was three weeks later, and he still had me in this sexual drought.

The exciting news was that I was in a good place, horny as hell, but still good.

A week after my mom was admitted to the hospital they released her, but in an unfortunate turn of events she had to return due to extreme dizziness and vomiting.

They had yet to make a diagnosis, but thankfully she was in good spirits. A few of her close friends had been visiting daily, and twice Merrick went with me to see her.

She liked him instantly, stating that he had a "good vibe about him."

Yup, that was my mom, alright. We were all about those vibes. I just needed her to get her meter checked in relation to Gary.

On an even better note, Gary hadn't shown his face in three weeks. My mom was a little worried if he was okay, but not too much because she said he'd done this disappearing act before, sometimes for a full month.

I never commented, but I knew that my mom was aware that I hoped Gary's absence would be permanent.

"How many cases did you close last quarter?" Merrick asked, studying the paperwork in his hands.

We had been in my office for two hours now. The first twenty minutes, I spent sucking his dick while being subjected to his erotically demeaning words. I enjoyed it so much that I almost came from the act alone.

"Um... forty-six," I said, trying to snap out of the haze.

I didn't have to think about the answer at all. I knew everything about every case like the back of my hand. The hesitation was due to how irresistible he was.

It was weird. All I had been doing for weeks was giving Merrick oral gratification, but still, I couldn't get enough of it. That made me wonder... *was I addicted to sex? Merrick? Or both?*

Likely the latter.

Merrick flipped pages and scribbled notes while I studied him. This meeting was for his benefit anyway. We had them once a month so that he remained informed of Dual's legal matters.

Without looking up, he asked, "Why are you staring at me like that, Jocelyn?"

My eyes quickly adjusted so that they were back on my files. I didn't need him to see me drooling over him. Although, apparently, he already had.

I cleared my throat. "I'm just in my thoughts, that's all."

Merrick thumbed to another page. "Uh-huh," he said, still focused on his work, "And would your thoughts have anything to do with me getting under that skirt?"

I sat up straighter, surprised by his comment. It was no secret that I was sexually wound up, but he usually didn't address it.

However, I would answer honestly. There was no point in lying because he could always tell.

Mind reading, bastard.

"Yes, sir," I admitted.

Merrick jotted down another note, then said, "In your mind, what am I doing?"

Of course, I understood the question; I just didn't want to

answer it. This had to be a trick. So instead, I let out a nervous laugh, feigning confusion. "What do you mean?"

"Are you daydreaming about me touching you?" he asked, his tone direct, leaving no room to dodge.

I licked my lips. "Yes."

Merrick finally closed the folder and rose from his chair, coming around the desk to stand in front of me.

"The meeting is over," he announced. "So why don't you take my hand and show me how I'm touching you."

I reached out to grab his hand, then paused.

Was he finally going to let me cum?

"Jocelyn," he said firmly. "I gave you an order."

Taking his hand, I pulled him toward me until he was leaning over my chair, with his hand resting on my pussy. His lips were inches away from mine and I had to fight with every fiber of my being not to kiss him.

Placing my hand over his, I pressed two of Merrick's fingers deep into my pussy, tilting my hips forward so that my clit rubbed up against his palm.

After gripping his wrist to hold his hand in place and accompanying it with my own movements, I found my rhythm.

My eyes fluttered shut, and my lips parted slightly. I needed this badly, and it felt so good. I was getting close, and it had only been a matter of seconds.

I guess being on edge for weeks would do that to you.

Merrick said nothing, and I really got into it. Moaning, groaning, and gripping the armrest with the hand that wasn't holding his in place. I could feel it. The presence of my sweet, glorious release was rounding the corner, and then... he snatched his hand away.

I almost cried. No exaggeration. There were about to be full-on tears and temper tantrums all over this office floor.

"Keep daydreaming," he said ruthlessly. "When I decide I

want you, I will have you, and not a moment sooner. At present, swallowing my cum is your only value to me. Do you understand?"

I almost cried. No exaggeration. There were about to be full-on tears and temper tantrums all over this office floor.

Crossing my legs, my chest rose and fell as I sucked in air.

"Yes, sir, I understand," I said aloud.

But on the inside, I was thinking he better be glad that a small, obviously insane, part of me loved being controlled by him, or else I would be flicking my bean all night once I left this office, giving myself the sexual release I'd been denied.

Merrick straightened, towering over me as I sat deprived and vibrating with need in my chair.

"Come to my place tonight," he said, heading toward the door. "I will need your services."

"Yes, sir," I replied respectfully, and then he was gone.

I sat on Merrick's couch, rubbing my toes over the buttery-soft carpet, waiting for him to finish a call. I'd arrived an hour ago, and after he let me in and told me to make myself at home, I hadn't seen him anymore.

There was a bar area in between the kitchen and living room that contained an impressive selection of alcohol, so I poured myself a glass of wine.

The sweet, dark flavor was so rich and crisp that ten minutes later, I sashayed back over and got another. I was now on my third... *or was it fourth?...* glass, and I felt liberated.

Merrick is going to get some top-notch head tonight. I giggled at the thought and buried my toes further into the carpet.

I giggled at the thought and buried my toes further into the carpet.

On the drive over I was frustrated about that stunt he pulled in his office. But now, I was ready to be a hedonist and party in the pleasures of being his submissive all night. I couldn't wait to get naked and feel his fingers in my hair, while I got lost in his moans.

Over the past weeks whenever I gave Merrick oral at his house we only did it in one of two places; his office while he worked or on the couch while he relaxed.

My fingers were crossed that tonight he'd choose the couch because this silky carpet felt wonderful when I was on my knees.

Then again, I liked when it happened in the office also because I got to wear my beloved nipple clamps.

Since most of his at-home work consisted of taking calls and attending virtual meetings, he used the clamps to direct how fast or slow I sucked him, just like he did that day in the restaurant.

Suddenly, Merrick entered the living room, and since I didn't notice any nipple clamps in his hand, I figured tonight, it would be the couch.

Sitting up, I set my almost-empty wine glass on the table.

He looked at it and then back at me.

"How many is that for you?" he asked.

I shrugged. "Third or fourth."

"And how do you feel?"

"I feel incredible," I admitted. "But I'm not drunk if that's what you're asking. Takes a lot more than wine to do that."

Merrick nodded slowly and said, "Are you ready to get started?"

"Absolutely, sir," I replied, toying with the top button on my shirt and about to assume my position on the floor, but he halted me.

"Not here. Come with me."

That's odd, I thought. *Then again, Merrick is unpredictable.*

I followed him upstairs to his bedroom not sure what to make of being there.

Had I earned my way back to his bed?

I would hate to think I did and all this turned out to be was him wanting me on my knees in a new location.

He removed his shirt and then started unbuttoning mine. I kept my hands at my sides, just as expected, and smiled up at him. Now that I'd had a few minutes, I realized that maybe the wine did have an effect because I felt extra giggly and playful.

"You have the best wine, sir."

Deep dimples appeared on his handsome face as he smiled back at me.

"You are absolutely gorgeous, do you know that?" he complimented.

"I have an idea," I replied sweetly.

Merrick's strong, gentle hands slid my shirt off my shoulders and down my arms. Once it fell to the floor, he reached around to unhook my bra.

"I have a surprise for you," he said.

My relaxed smile turned into a full-on grin. "For me?! Why?"

"You've done well these past few weeks. Every request I made you honored, and every demand I gave you completed with obedience and respect, including opening up to me, and I know how hard that was for you."

The fact that he understood that opening up was hard for me had me speechless and misty-eyed.

Alright, Jocelyn, I thought to myself. *No more wine-drinking at his house if it makes you this emotional.*

Merrick discarded my bra like it was a nuisance and his hands dropped to my skirt.

"Tonight is all about you," he continued. "I am going to let you run the show."

Uh oh, was this another trap?

"What does that mean?" I asked cautiously.

I was now naked and so was he.

"You'll see," Merrick said.

Getting into bed, he relaxed back onto the pillow, his hands behind his head. My mind returned to the first night I met him. Merrick was stretched out like he was now, looking like temptation on a platter and I walked out of the hotel room expecting to never see him again.

I couldn't believe that night was only a little over ten months ago. It seemed like forever. I... no, we had come so far.

My body reacted when he was near, his needs had become my own and I understood, even without words, his expectations of me.

Yet, right now, I was drawing a blank. I wasn't comprehending what he wanted me to do.

"Why are you just standing there?" Merrick asked.

"I'm a little lost, sir," I said. "Aren't you going to tie me up?"

"Nope," he replied simply.

What the hell? Maybe I am drunk," I thought.

I stood there like an idiot because I had to be missing something. Merrick always tied me up or, at least, instructed me on where I could or could not put my hands.

Now there were no orders or instructions.

His eyes were fixed on the ceiling, and my hands shot to my hips. The sassiness and skepticism within me spilled out. This was a trick, like in the office earlier today.

"So... you aren't going to tell me what I can and can't do?"

"Nope," he repeated.

Alright. I'll play his game. I knew how to get him talking.

"Mr. Alexander, are you saying that tonight you are my submissive?"

The look he gave had me regretting the question. It was a warning not to test him and I heard it loud and clear. "I am no ones submissive," he said pointedly.

I nodded then threw up my hands. I needed another drink.

"What are you then?" I asked.

"I'm running out of patience if you don't get your sexy ass over here."

Welp, no need to threaten me with a good time.

I straddled him, the thrill of what was taking place and my lowered inhibitions causing my hands to roam his chest and abs at lightning speed.

Part of me believed this was a test and any minute now, he would tell me to stop or to go and sit in the corner for failing, but he didn't say anything.

His hands remained behind his head and he watched me with a pleased expression.

I paused from enjoying the hands-on intimacy and said, "Why the change-up tonight?"

"It takes us to a new level. You. Are. Mine," he said, articulating each word, the meaning of his intent unmistakable.

My heart took over. I wasn't prepared for what I said next, didn't even think I would say it, but from my lips came the truth, "I think I have always been yours."

I kissed him, my hands sliding around his neck and my body pressing closer against his. The way I felt was hard to explain. I wavered between free and afraid of what my confession meant, but nothing would stop me from enjoying this.

I explored his body with my hands and tongue for a while, then decided it was time to fully enjoy this ride.

Carefully, I moved upward until my pussy was almost at his face. Placing one knee on either side of his head, I looked down at him. He hadn't moved an inch and still somehow managed to look completely relaxed and in control.

"Any famous last words?" I teased.

Merrick licked his lips, the action so hot my pussy pulsated. Then his gaze locked with mine and he said, "Don't go easy on me."

"Don't go easy on me."

I dove in—or rather, he did. His tongue moved with slow intention, exploring and consuming me, sending sensation rippling through my body.

Every so often, I lifted myself up enough to tease him, hovering just out of reach for several seconds before lowering myself again... down... down... down... until the soft brush of his lips met my center once more.

Then I would rotate my hips, glazing his mouth with my juices.

Wrapping my fingers around the top of his high-end tufted headboard, I rode his face like a professional cowgirl with her eyes set on the first-place trophy.

At one point, I was grinding so hard against his face that I wasn't sure he could breathe, but I took the fact that he was sucking and rolling his tongue as proof that there was still life down there.

I came in an overwhelming rush, my thighs tightening around his face and my cries of ecstasy filling the room as Merrick practically sucked the orgasm out of me.

He was intense and for the millionth time, I wondered, *where did this man get his skills?*

Arching my back, impassioned cries broke free as I thrashed against his mouth. He abruptly relocated his hands from behind his head and wrapped his arms around my waist, drawing me closer.

Damn, if I got any deeper into his mouth, eating me out would no longer be a figure of speech.

With ease, Merrick lifted me off him and flipped me over onto my back. After wiping his mouth, he pushed my legs wide and settled himself in between.

Instead of immediately ramming his manhood into me as I'd hoped, his intense eyes found mine.

"Look down and watch me enter you," he demanded.

My eyes dropped to his dick, currently hovering near my entrance. It was an erotic sight as I watched and felt him disappear into me inch by inch.

Once he was almost fully planted inside, Merrick pushed forward hard, driving his dick the rest of the way.

I moaned in satisfaction, locking my legs around his powerful, tight body.

"That's it," he urged. "I want to hear every moan, every whimper, every fucking sigh. Don't hold back on me."

I couldn't hold back if I tried. Three weeks of pent-up sexual frustration was being forced out of me by a man that held all the codes. He did things to my body that exposed my secrets, my fears and my very soul.

"Did you miss this?" Merrick whispered into my ear, his tone cocky.

My voice was breathless and thin as he slammed into me harder and deeper. "Yes, sir."

"Have you learned your lesson?"

"Yes, oh fuck, yes!" I shouted.

He hit a sweet spot and my back sunk into the firm, yet soft mattress. I fisted the sheets with one hand and squeezed Merrick's arm with the other. I was traveling into that euphoric zone that only he had the power to send me to.

"Both hands on me," he ordered. Once I complied, he said, "Now, what do I want from you?"

"Everything," I cried, my body shaking, my pussy clenching, my fingers tightening.

"And what will you do about that?"

"I'll obey! I will give you everything, sir. I won't... hold... back!" I half squealed, half screamed.

There was nothing mild about my orgasms with Merrick.

They were extreme and made me feel like a wild animal he needed to tame, but since tonight he was letting me roam free, I clung to him, desperate and undone, biting his neck, all restraint gone.

That's it, gorgeous," He whispered, urging me on as I dug my nails deep enough into his back to draw blood. "Let go."

Merrick wanted me to unleash all my hurt, all my pain, and all my desire, and I did just that.

Surrendering completely as the moment overtook me. I couldn't get enough of him, and I knew in that instant that he felt the same about me.

Shit! Those were deep, I thought to myself as I lay against Merrick's chest, my gaze fixed on the teeth marks I'd left on his neck.

My fingers tenderly traced the shallow impressions, and I winced at the sight. I hadn't broken the skin, thankfully, but even so, it still looked painful.

"I'm sorry," I said. "Are you okay? Does it hurt?"

Merrick took my hand and lowered it back to his chest before he resumed gently stroking my arm. Ignoring my question, he asked, "Did you enjoy yourself, beautiful?"

I shook my head and laughed a little.

That's the Merrick I knew. When my concern was about him, he always made it about me.

I brushed a quick kiss over the marks on his neck before straddling him. Planting my hands flat against his chest, I looked down at him and grinned.

"I absolutely enjoyed it! I've told you before, your dick is amazing. You've even *almost* made up for the three-week torture you put me under," I said playfully.

Merrick scoffed. "You were hardly the only one suffering through those three weeks."

I rolled my eyes. "Oh, please. I'm sure it was so unbearable for you getting your dick sucked every day, while I was denied any sort of release," I said sarcastically.

Something in his gaze shifted then, and the teasing warmth faded, replaced by a heat that made my breath catch. He looked at me like he was deciding exactly how he planned to remind me who really had the upper hand.

Merrick slid a hand down between my legs and gently caressed my pussy. I moaned instantly, his simple touch awakening my need for him yet again.

When he spoke, his voice was calm on the surface, but edged with authority.

"If you think not being able to be inside you," he said, pressing a finger into me, deliberately slow, "or not being able to taste you—" He withdrew the finger, then lifted it to his mouth and licked off my wetness, never breaking eye contact. "—wasn't torture for me, then you severely underestimate just how addicted I am to you."

I searched his face for a hint of teasing, but there was none, only certainty, and that realization left me trembling and turned the fuck on.

"Maybe we need a round two, just to make sure your thirst is properly quenched," I said suggestively.

"I agree," Merrick replied, equally flirtatious. "But first I need to tell you about your surprise."

I stared at him, perplexed. "My surprise wasn't the mind-blowing sex we just had?"

Merrick laughed and shook his head. "No. The surprise is that I am ready to take you on that date I asked you for."

"Okay," I said hesitantly, glancing at the clock. "It's 11 p.m., but I'm down. What do you have in mind?"

Merrick sat up and slid out of bed. I admired his naked body, pausing at his impressive length. He waited until my eyes met his again before he spoke.

He was so smug.

"Breakfast," he said.

I was fine with breakfast for dinner, but Merrick didn't strike me as that type of guy.

"At this hour?" I asked, getting out of bed also.

"Well, the place we're going isn't open yet, but it will be by the time we get there," he replied.

"And where exactly is there?" I inquired looking up at him.

Taking my hand and pulling me along, he said, "Come join me in the shower for round two, and I'll tell you all about it."

Chapter Fourteen

Merrick took me to Paris. And not Paris avenue, the name of the street a few blocks from where I grew up, but Paris, the city in France where the food was artful, high-quality, exquisite and unforgettable.

Who does that for a first date?

I guess Merrick did, and he did so in his private jet. My mind was blown.

We left around midnight, and although the flight was only six hours, when we arrived in Paris, it was almost noon their time, but Merrick had promised me breakfast and he delivered.

The first place he took me to was Laurent Duchêne. They not only had golden, buttery croissants that tasted sublime, Laurent carried additional treats such as pastries, macaroons, cakes and chocolates.

We enjoyed our breakfast with lavender tea, my favorite, at a nearby park and from there we did some sightseeing. Merrick was familiar with the area as he'd been to Paris quite a few times, so as usual, he led, and I followed.

The Latin Quarter was our first stop. It was a charming neighborhood with winding streets and great places to explore.

It's home to Sorbonne University, one of the oldest

colleges in Europe, and Pantheon, an architectural wonder that was originally a church, but now contains the tombs of famous French figures.

There were also several adorable shops and fabulous boutiques nearby and Merrick took me to each one and bought me something.

By the time I was done, I had two designer purses, several stylish scarves, five pairs of heels, and a necklace with matching earrings.

I wanted to purchase a few things because, it's Paris! But I also wanted to support some of the local businesses. Nevertheless, since Merrick doesn't like me spending my own money when I'm with him, he paid for it all.

We continued our stroll, talking, laughing and drinking hot chocolate as I took in all the sights. Several times we took walking breaks at various parks and gardens where I got glimpses of the Eiffel Tower far off in the distance.

Then, we stopped to have lunch at Les Deux Magots, a classic cafe frequented by artists and writers, including Hemingway and Picasso.

From there, museums, shops, cathedrals, chatting with locals and romantic boat rides, where we spent most of the time kissing, filled our day.

Eventually, we made it to the Eiffel Tower, but we didn't get to explore the inside because we didn't have reservations. Merrick promised that if I wanted to go inside, he would make the reservation and bring us back.

However, that wasn't necessary. Simply being this close to it had me in awe. The view from the street was stunning. The wrought iron design loomed over us with a beauty that words could not describe.

It was getting dark, so all the bright lights made the tower a magnificent glossy gold. It was an experience I will never forget and since I took a million photos, I'm sure I never would.

Plus, after spending the whole day kissing Merrick and seeing the structure that inspired the bondage position he used on me, I was ready to pull off my tourist shirt and let Merrick... tour me.

Our last stop was dinner at Epicure, an upscale hotel restaurant that specialized in French fine dining & wine. It was breathtakingly romantic and the perfect way to end our first date.

I had never walked so much in my life and I loved every minute of it.

Back at the jet, Merrick's staff awaited us. Julian, the flight attendant, collected our bags and helped us get situated for take-off.

We spent the first hour in silence while Merrick checked emails and I stared out the window, pinching myself ever so often to ensure this was real.

The jet was lavish, falling in line with everything Merrick owned. It seated up to eight passengers and included an elegant bathroom, dining space, kitchen and mini bar. Merrick and I sat on a long, leather sofa with dark oak wood trim and tables that connected to it on either side.

Merrick closed his laptop and pushed the adjustable square tray that it rested on to the far right side. He shifted to face me on the couch, stretching one arm out across the top behind me.

"I apologize for being occupied since we boarded. I had a few work matters that couldn't wait."

I waved him off.

"No one understands work demands better than me. Is there anything you need me to do?"

"No, but I should inform you that Shelia quit a few weeks ago and things have gotten messy."

It dawned on me that I hadn't seen Shelia for a while. Since we barely talked her absence hadn't stood out to me.

"Was there an issue? Why did she quit?"

"I don't think she and Ashton were seeing eye to eye about..." he trailed off.

"The contract?" I offered.

"Yes, but Ashton and I are handling it."

He sighed. I could tell this Shelia thing must have gotten ugly, but I wouldn't poke into Ashton's personal affairs.

"No more talk about work," he said. "All of my attention belongs to you."

I scooted closer.

"Well now, you just made my night even better."

Our lips were like opposite pole magnets, attracting the touch of the other whenever they were near. The heat and passion in this kiss burned as strong as always and I was left breathless and yearning.

"I still can't believe you have a private jet. Is this what you use for client meetings?"

"No. Outside of the agreement I have with you, I am very strict about not mixing business with pleasure. I fly commercial business class for those meetings and at this point, I have racked up so many points and rewards I don't think I even pay for those flights anymore."

Merrick was fascinating to me as well as intelligent, kind, arrogant, and selfless. How was one man so complex?

"There is a lot I don't know about you," I said.

"That's a fair assessment and one that I hope to change. Tell me, what do you want to know?"

"Just like that?" I said. "I can ask you anything?"

"Just like that," he responded.

"And you will answer?"

"I will answer, Jocelyn."

He was serious and from his body language, he was

preparing himself. Merrick knew I was going for the jugular. I'd shared my deepest, darkest secrets. Now, it was his turn.

"What happened that changed you as a Dom?"

He faced forward, rested his head against the couch and closed his eyes. I studied him, positive that he wasn't going to answer.

"I almost killed my sub," he said.

What the shit?!... I meant... hell, the what?! I shook my head to clear it. My thoughts were incomprehensible.

Did Merrick say he almost killed his sub? Wait! Did he even say almost? Was his sub dead?

My heart was pounding so hard I couldn't tell if the vibrations were coming from the light turbulence we were experiencing or from me.

"Could you repeat that, please?" I said.

"I almost killed my sub."

Yup. That's what I thought he said. At least I could take solace in the fact that he said "almost" before the word killed.

I dreaded asking, but I needed to know.

"What did she do that made you want to kill her?"

He chuckled to himself, but there was no real amusement in it.

"It wasn't like that. We were doing breath play. You know, choking? Erotic asphyxiation? Either way, it got out of hand."

My thudding heart settled down in my chest. Hearing that it wasn't intentional made a big difference.

"You could have led with that you know?"

"I don't like to talk about it."

I got that. If I almost ended someone's life, I imagine I wouldn't like to talk about it either.

"I understand. Take your time."

Merrick let out a long exhale.

"Blair was my sub for three years, and we'd built a great deal of mutual trust between each other. It was normal for me not to see her for a few weeks at a time due to our busy lives, so when she showed up at the club wanting to do a scene after a month, I didn't think anything of it."

He swallowed, staring into the distance, traveling back to a memory that I knew he wanted to keep buried. I covered his hand with my own, offering him the little support I could.

"What happened?" I asked.

"Ten seconds is what happened."

I tilted my head quizzically. "Sorry, I'm not following."

Merrick released another long weary sigh. "Choking was Blair's favorite and we did it often. As her Dom, I had come to learn her limits and Blair could safely withstand ten seconds of air restriction."

My brow furrowed. "Ten seconds doesn't seem like a long time to hold your breath," I said.

"It is when someone is cutting off your air supply for you."

"When you put it that way..." I replied, my words stopping short as I reimagined the scene.

Merrick picked up where he left off.

"Normally, I watched her, paying attention to her expressions and responses as a fail-safe, but this time I closed my eyes, allowing myself to get lost in the moment a little, and counted to ten in my head."

I covered my mouth, nerves on edge and terrified for Blair, which made no sense because I already knew the outcome, she survived, but my pulse wasn't behaving.

"When I looked down, she'd passed out and I immediately called 9-1-1."

Now I, too, was staring straight ahead. Off into the distance. "Wow, that's scary."

"And also unforgivable," he said.

Was that anger in his voice?

My head snapped in his direction. I was confused again. My emotions were all over the place.

"Are you saying you blame her?"

"No," he replied flatly. "I take full responsibility for anything that happens on my watch, but a heads-up would have been nice. I was devastated about what I'd done. I kept racking my brain, trying to figure out what went wrong. I was 100% positive I had not restricted her air supply beyond the ten seconds. Eyes closed or not, I am very careful with my timing."

Julian came over to see if we needed anything. We both shook our heads and once he was out of earshot, Merrick resumed.

"A week later, Blair called to confess. She had begun taking medication due to sudden heart issues, and one of the possible side effects is shortness of breath. According to her doctor, the medicine, adrenaline, and pressure on her neck would have made her pass out within a few seconds."

My eyes went wide. Dammit! Now I was angry at Blair as if I were the one involved in this unfortunate mishap. *Blair should have told us this!*

"That's horrible! Why didn't she tell you?"

"She thought she could get away with it. In her mind, if she could handle our scenes before the meds and diagnosis, why not after? Her goal was to feel normal again, and she kept it from me because she feared if I knew, I wouldn't have gone through with it."

"Was she right?" I asked.

"Abso-fucking-lutely! Breath play or any scene for that matter already carries a risk. Doing so with drugs in your system is dangerous and irresponsible."

I felt horrible for him.

"Merrick, you have to know that's not your fault."

He shook his head. "Whose fault it is changes nothing. I could have killed her."

"Did she remain your sub?"

"She wanted to, but I refused." His eyes found mine again. "That was five years ago."

"That's a long time. Do you miss it? The more extreme stuff, I mean?"

"No. Or at least I thought I didn't, but what happened in your office was a knee-jerk reaction. So maybe, after all these years, I have been holding back."

I could never forget the day he choked me in the office for being disrespectful. It was such a turn-on. It was something I kept hoping would happen again.

"If it makes you feel any better," I said quietly. "You don't have to hold back. I trust you and you can trust me."

He turned fully towards me and stared.

"What are you saying, Jocelyn?"

I sucked in a deep breath and nibbled at my bottom lip. "I'm saying that I want to try kinkier, rougher things with you." Merrick looked taken aback. "Not immediately," I added, "but... I'd like you to train me to get there."

"Are you sure about that?"

"Yes, sir. I love being your sub, and eventually, I want you to have complete sexual control over me."

"That doesn't scare you?" he asked, his fingers caressing my face.

I placed my hand on the back of his and rested my cheek in the palm of his hand.

"No. There is something about serving you that comes naturally to me. Plus, I love how dirty you make me feel," I said mischievously.

He gave me a sly grin, his tone lighter than it had been the previous ten minutes when he said, "As I told you before, Jocelyn, that's because you're a whore. You were made for it and you're good at it."

I quivered, his words arousing me.

"Mmm," I moaned. "You know how to get me going."

"Good, it gives me more control," he said possessively. "As far as training you to do more goes... I'll think about it. In the meantime, stand up and take off your dress."

I glanced up, my eyes finding Julian. He was in a corner stacking blankets on a shelf.

I wasn't wearing a bra or underwear, so once I removed the dress, visually speaking, it was a free-for-all.

"Hey," Merrick said, getting my attention. "Eyes on me, and do what you're told."

"Yes, sir."

Getting off the couch, I pulled my dress over my head. Merrick held out his hand and I gave it to him. He placed it in a small drawer that I hadn't noticed underneath the couch.

"You don't need clothes. This is how you will remain for the rest of the flight. Put your hands behind your back."

"Yes, sir. Anything else?"

"You open your legs without hesitation whenever I want. That's good enough for now."

I smiled flirtatiously.

"Don't forget about my mouth, sir. I'll also gladly open it whenever you need to use it."

"Oh, I haven't forgotten about that pretty little mouth. That's where I plan to finish after I'm done fucking you today."

I licked my lips, already able to taste him. He made a come hither motion with his finger and I went to sit on his lap.

Gazing into his eyes I said, "You are so good to me, sir."

"That is because you earned it."

It had been a long week and I'd earned many things.

Therefore, spending the rest of the flight earning my way into the 'Mile High Club' was a welcomed bonus.

I placed a robe, socks, and undergarments in the red duffle bag and zipped it up. My mom was still in the hospital, not doing as well as we'd hoped, but still smiling.

I skimmed the room, ensuring I didn't forget any of the requested items when I remembered her shampoo. She said the one at the hospital was too drying and stripped her curls of their usual lushness.

After picking up the shampoo, I made a last-minute decision to grab the conditioner as well. She didn't ask for it, but I was certain she would appreciate having it.

Immediately after closing the bag a second time, I heard a noise. I turned towards the bedroom door.

Nothing, or more importantly, no one, was there. However, a few heartbeats later, I heard it again.

Was someone in the kitchen?

My mom was in the hospital, and Gary had been MIA for weeks. No one should be here but me.

Quickly and quietly, I searched for something to defend myself with, in case it was necessary but found nothing.

My mom was a minimalist and in her sixties. Unless my goal was to spray the intruder with a collection of floral scents, dress them in an outfit that was out of fashion, or tuck them into bed tightly with grandmas quilts while I made my escape, I was out of luck.

I picked up the bag and prayed that it was Gary.

Imagine that, hoping to see the monster you knew, versus the one you didn't.

Moving down the hall towards the stairs, I held my breath,

fearing the intruder had supersonic ears, and every breath I took was a dead giveaway to my location.

I walked sideways like I'd seen ninjas do in movies. To my relief and dismay, another noise rang out – this one was an unmistakable curse from an intoxicated Gary.

I exhaled, adjusted the bag on my shoulder and went to the kitchen. Gary was at the table. A beer bottle in hand and two empty ones on the counter.

Removing the bag from my shoulder and placing it on the counter a rotten smell assaulted my nostrils. I held my breath, fighting hard to avoid inhaling too much of his musty odor.

Didn't he just get here? I wondered. *How were two bottles of beer already empty? And how long had it been since the man showered?*

Gary's jeans and shirt were covered in stains, and his ever-growing beer belly peeked out from under his shirt. I swore every time I saw him it had doubled in size.

I watched him out of my peripheral as I moved toward the pantry. Gary actually wasn't a bad-looking guy, but his current poor hygiene, combined with the fact that he used and abused my mom, made him the ugliest man alive in my book.

Even still, I'd never seen him like this. He looked terrified, angry and defeated all at the same time.

Not my problem.

I ignored him, my insides seething with rage that he had returned.

Why won't he stay away? For that matter, why won't my mom kick him out? He isn't doing her any good.

Opening the pantry door, I checked for snacks. My eyes landed on crackers and granola bars and I collected the goodies and added them to the luggage.

"So you're going to act like you don't see me sitting here?" Gary said.

I continued checking the contents of the bag as if he hadn't spoken. I think I had everything.

"Where's your mom?"

His questions fell on deaf ears. He didn't deserve a response, but once he blurted out, "She broke her own arm, you know? And if she says any different the bitch is lying on me." He got one.

Facing him, I said, "Why don't you leave, Gary? You've been gone for over a month now. Why come back?"

"This is my home," he spat. The saliva pooling around his mouth made my stomach turn. "I have a right to be here and if you don't like it that's your fucking problem."

He took another swig of beer, slamming it back on the table once he was done.

"I never liked you," I said. "One day, my mom will realize how worthless you are and that day can't come soon enough."

With extreme effort, Gary unsteadily got to his feet.

"Yap, yap, yap, just like your mom. I don't want to hear any of that shit. I need some money. When is she coming home?"

He was now moving towards me.

"That is none of your business," I said, defiantly.

"Alright then, since you want to be your mother's keeper, you give me some money. Hell, it would save me the time of rummaging through her purse and taking the scraps she has," he added with a sardonic laugh.

I shook my head.

"You're an asshole," I said. "Your free ride is over."

I intended to grab the bag and head out the door, but Gary, moving much faster than I expected, rushed toward me, fist in the air.

"Who do you think you're talking to!" he yelled.

I shielded my face just in time, avoiding a blow that landed on my shoulder.

It hurt, but I wasted no time dwelling on the pain. Gary was about to strike me again and I had to react fast.

My fingers locked around one of the empty bottles, and I hit him as hard as I could. It connected with the side of his head and shattered.

Gary grunted and fell, holding his head. I spotted blood oozing past his hand, but he didn't seem to notice. He was apoplectic with rage, placing his palms on the floor and pushing himself up.

Maybe it was true what they said about drunk people not feeling pain. Well, I wasn't drunk and I felt everything. My shoulder was on fire, my nerves were shot and adrenaline was flooding my body by the truckload.

Even though I wanted to, I had enough sense to know that I couldn't beat Gary in a fight, so not sparing him another glance, I yanked up the bag and got my ass out of there.

Chapter Fifteen

"THIS IS MY RED ROSE!"

My back was to the bathroom mirror and I was holding up a second mirror in front of me.

It was only a handheld mirror, which meant it offered me a limited view of the injury, but what I could see proved what I'd already known; the bruise looked horrendous and Gary was an indolent incompetent asshole.

I hoped that hit to the head killed him, but I'm sure I wasn't that lucky.

I lowered the mirror and cursed. The purplish-blue contusion around my shoulder was easily visible on my brown skin, and even now, three days later, it still hurt.

No one knew about the incident between Gary and I. I didn't tell my mom when I dropped off her items, hadn't confided in Jada when we talked yesterday and Merrick was out of town. Although even if he were here, I wouldn't share this with him.

No, this was my fight and Gary had to go. The problem was I hadn't figured out how to make that happen, but I would.

"Shit!" I shrieked, noticing the time. "I'm late."

Dropping the mirror on the bathroom counter, I finished getting ready and rushed out of the door. I was conducting a meeting this morning with the legal team to check everyone's progress on their cases and assign new ones.

When I arrived at the office, everyone (including Ashton) was already in the conference room waiting for me. He and Merrick sat in on meetings when they could, but that wasn't very often. It figures that the day I ran late, he would be there.

Apologizing to everyone, I began the meeting. Thankfully I prepared ahead and had folders ready for the team to follow along.

After two hours of clarifying, assigning, reviewing and working through past, present and future cases, I concluded the meeting.

"Does anyone have any questions?"

One of my paralegals, Janie, raised her hand.

"I'm sorry to have to do this during the meeting, but I figured this would be the best time. My son is having surgery on the 23rd of next month and I won't be able to attend the hearing on the Theodore Blakey case with you. I was wondering if maybe someone else here could go instead?"

Janie looked around worried and hopeful, but no one said anything. I didn't fault them because everyone in this room had a significant workload already.

"It's okay, Janie. I think I'll be able to get through that one without assistance. Will you have all the evidence organized by then?"

"I will, I promise," Janie stated.

"In that case..." the door opened, and in walked Merrick. Several heads turned to watch as he quietly made his way to the back of the conference room and took a seat. I turned toward Janie. "there are no issues. I'll take care of it. I hope everything goes well with your son and please let me know if there is anything I can do for you."

Janie thanked me profusely, and I dismissed everyone and

returned to my office. Ten minutes after settling in, there was a knock at my door. It was Merrick in all his sexiness and swag.

"Hi," I said with a smile. "I thought you weren't due back until the end of the week."

"The client had to postpone, so I went home, showered, answered some emails, and here I am," he said, his deep voice provoking lust to flare within me.

"Guess I'm lucky."

"I was thinking the same thing," he said.

He takes off his suit jacket and tosses it over a chair. Then, coming around my desk, Merrick offers me his hand and pulls me into his arms.

"I apologize for being late. Did I miss any important updates or instructions for the cases?"

I breathed in his scent, notes of mint and cedar wood easily identifiable to me thanks to my love for candles. I never got tired of how easily my stress lessened in his presence.

"There is nothing new. You are all caught up."

Merrick ran his hands over my breasts, caressing my nipples through the thin fabric.

"Do you have any meetings or calls you need to take care of right now?" he asked.

Our voices were whispers and our desires were breaking through to the surface.

"No, Mr. Alexander, I am free for the next twenty minutes."

"In that case," he said, lifting my chin. "It's, sir."

Business was over. Playtime had arrived.

"Yes, sir, where do you want me?"

"On your knees."

"My pleasure."

Settling myself on the floor, I stared up at him. I reached up to trace my fingers over his belt, waiting for his orders to begin. Instead of speaking, he runs his fingers through my hair because whenever he notices I am too eager, he makes me wait to please him.

Placing his hands on my shoulders, Merrick pulled me forward so that I was closer, but the sudden pressure on my bruise caused me to wince and recoil from his grasp.

Quickly, I tried to recover and steady myself, but I wasn't fast enough.

"Stand up," he said, taking a step back, his brows furrowed.

Fuck, fuck, fuck, shit!

When I'm on my feet, Merrick loosens the top buttons on my shirt, slides it down my shoulders, and turns me around.

I didn't have to wonder how he knew. If the way I flinched in pain wasn't enough to tip him off, the lumpiness of my swollen shoulder was.

His touch is tender and careful as he inspects the bruise. The concern in his voice is heavy when he says, "What happened to you?"

I pulled my shirt back up and faced him, convinced that if he wasn't looking at the bruise, he could forget about it and move on faster.

"I don't know," I said, reaching to touch it off instinct. "I think I bumped into something."

"What did you bump into?"

Of course, he would have a follow-up question that I was not prepared for. I was so busy making sure my acting skills of "it's no biggie" were Oscar-worthy that I wasn't planning ahead.

However, I couldn't think of an answer fast enough, so what did I do? I said the dumbest thing imaginable.

"You know what? It may have happened the last time we did something. We get kind of rough. Maybe I didn't notice it at the time."

Why did I say that?!

As soon as the shipment of words left my lips, I knew they would sink. Now, Merrick knew I was lying and that gave him a reason to be suspicious.

Crossing his arms, he narrowed his gaze.

"I don't leave bruises on you, and I know every inch of your body, so try again."

I did not want him involved. This was not his fight. It was mine. My mental wheels were spinning, searching, constructing and rehearsing a response to get me out of the spotlight, but when Merrick said, "Is this your way of proving to me that I can trust you?" all production came to a halt.

I'd told him on the plane that he could trust me as it pertained to my limits, but this wasn't the same... was it?

"That's different and you know it. I don't want you involved, Merrick."

"Involved with what?"

I exhaled and went to lean on my desk.

"I got into a small altercation with my stepdad," I confessed, "but I have it under control."

Rage filled Merrick's eyes. "Where is he?"

I straightened and squared my shoulders, but the effort caused the swollen side to sink back down almost immediately, making my attempt to put my foot down look lopsided.

"Merrick, are you listening? Stay out of this. It has nothing to do with you."

"Where is he?" Merrick restated. His usual calm tone appeared colder than I'd thought possible.

"At first, I was asking you to stay out of this now, I'm telling you," I cautioned, my voice rising. "I do not need your help."

Merrick pulled out his phone and hit some buttons.

"7285 Lynnfield Way. That's your mom's address, right?"

Dammit! He'd taken me by there several times to pick up

things for her since she had been in the hospital, and now my letting him get too close was coming back to bite me in the ass.

I appreciated his concern for me, and his outrage on my behalf touched my heart in ways I'd never felt before, but I didn't need him coming to my rescue. I would find a way to take care of Gary. I just needed time.

Merrick grabbed his jacket and headed for the door. For him this conversation was over, for me it was just getting started.

"This is my red rose!" I shouted, stepping forward. "I do not need saving. I am not Blair." Merrick froze his hand on the doorknob, but he didn't turn around. "This is my line in the sand," I said.

Merrick released the knob and came toward me, his anger so strong it filled the room.

"I guess you better draw a new fucking line," he said before exiting my office.

After work, I drove to Merrick's house. My mind was racing, and so was my car, as I ran through several red lights. It was late, 11:05 pm, according to my dashboard.

After our heated disagreement, I tried to get out of the office as quickly as possible. Unfortunately, several meetings and work obligations caused my ability to leave to be delayed.

Merrick not only hadn't answered any of my calls, he hadn't returned to the office, and being left in the dark about an issue that pertained to me, made my blood boil.

All day I wrestled with conflicting thoughts and emotions on this entire scenario.

Did he find Gary? If so, what did he do to him? Did it even matter? Gary deserves every unfortunate thing coming to him.

Why was I even surprised that Merrick came to my defense? Would I rather he have done nothing at all?"

"Shit!" I shouted, hitting the steering wheel.

My eyes glistened with tears. I felt so jumbled that I wasn't sure which emotion they were stemming from.

Why couldn't Merrick stay out of it? I did not need him or any man to fight my battles. Protecting myself was all I knew... it was all I had. How dare he take that away from me.

I pulled into his driveway and hurried toward the door. I didn't remember turning off the car, but when I looked down, my keys were in my hand, and when I looked back up, Merrick was holding the front door open.

He stepped out of the way while I wordlessly stormed my way in. He was expecting me and I was ready to get this over with.

Merrick closed the door behind me and the first thing I noticed was his resigned expression.

He was wearing blue sweatpants and a matching shirt, holding a glass of dark liquid, which I guessed to be bourbon, his favorite drink for unwinding. Then, I noticed the soft jazz playing in the background, *our* favorite way of unwinding and my heart felt heavy.

I took in everything about him, from his stance to the way his eyes spoke to me. Assuming this would be the last time I saw him in this environment, I never wanted to forget it.

Taking a seat on the couch, Merrick placed his glass on the table and leaned back.

"Would you like anything?" he asked, not looking at me.

"Yes, Merrick, I would like some answers. What did you do?"

Appearing utterly exhausted, he sat forward to take a sip from the glass and then resumed his previous position.

"I took care of Gary," he said.

I waited, but that was all he was going to give me. My

stomach tightened, and for a brief instant, I imagined the worst.

"What do you mean took care of him?"

Merrick shook his head slightly, his eyes closed and a muscle in his jaw ticked.

"He isn't sleeping with the fishes if that's what you're asking. But he got the message and he won't be bothering you or your mom again."

"Did you... hurt him?" I asked, almost afraid to hear the answer.

I didn't like Gary. Actually, I loathed the man, but that didn't mean I wanted to be responsible for dragging Merrick into this and possibly getting him into trouble.

Merrick got to his feet, his jaw clenched and eyes intense.

"I wanted to hurt him, Jocelyn. Hell, I wanted to kill him, but the man is what, in his 60's? Plus, he is already deep in a pile of dangerous shit."

"Dangerous... how?"

"He owes Stone Lucchese a lot of money."

I'd never heard of that name before.

"Who is Stone Lucchese? A business partner of yours or something?"

"Hell no! Stone is no associate of mine, but I know of him. There is no way you climb the ladder of building what I have without at least being aware of some of the wealthiest men that are on the wrong side of the law."

"Wait, I'm lost. Why does Gary owe Stone money? And what does that have to do with any of this?" I asked, not sure I wanted to know.

"Your stepdad is heavy into gambling and he made some promises to pay, that he didn't keep, to the wrong man."

"How do you know this?"

Merrick laughed, a sound that held no humor, only pity and distaste.

"Oh, he told me. While he practically begged me not to kill him for what he'd done to you and your mom."

I couldn't say it didn't all make sense. When I last saw Gary, I could tell something had changed. He was terrified and desperate, now I knew why, but why did Merrick believe him?

"How do you know he wasn't lying to you?"

"Doesn't matter," Merrick said pointedly. "It's a risk I am not willing to take. From what I know about Stone, he isn't above killing the loved ones of those that owe him money simply to make a point. Therefore, Gary needs to stay far away from you both. So I offered him an out and he accepted it."

"You gave him money?" I asked, my eyes widening. I hated this, hated that Merrick was pulled into my mess, and hated that he didn't listen in the first place. "How much?"

"Enough to pay off his debt and get his ass out of town. With the promise that if I ever see him again, the outcome wouldn't be pleasant."

Those conflicting emotions from earlier had amplified. Merrick may have saved me and my mom's life. I should be eternally grateful for that, but I was still having trouble coming to grips with the fact that he inserted himself into this at all.

It wasn't only about his total disregard for my wishes, he could have been killed. With Gary already on the edge, what if he had a gun and when Merrick showed up, he thought it was one of Stone's men and got trigger-happy?

"I told you to stay out of it," I finally said, exhaustion now obvious in my voice as well. "but you were so set on being the hero that you acted as if you didn't even hear me."

"I heard you. I just chose to ignore it."

Merrick's reply showcased his usual stubbornness and gave my irritation new footing.

"And that's the problem! You completely dismissed what I wanted."

In a few long strides, he was in front of me.

"Jocelyn," he said, reaching to touch my face, but I turned away. Merrick let his hand fall to his side. "I love you and I respect you, but I will always cross the line if it means protecting you."

I blinked several times and stepped back. Did he just say... that he loved me?

No, no, no, no, no.

"Don't do that. Don't tell me you love me, using it as an excuse for what you did. You don't love me, you love fucking me."

Merrick's eyes searched mine. "Does lying about how you feel make it easier for you?" he asked quietly. "You already know how I feel about you and I know you feel it too."

I broke eye contact. "I don't feel anything," I lied.

Merrick turned away, shaking his head. He sat down, lifted his hands to his head and massaged his temples. "Fine, Jocelyn, keep telling yourself that," he said in a defeated tone.

"What I feel," *I paused and started again,* "What I felt for you doesn't matter. I can't simply brush off what you did."

"I don't expect you to. If you did, you wouldn't be the woman I love."

There was that word again, love.

"Are you even sorry?" I asked.

"Not even a little," he said.

I let out a long sigh.

"Alright then, I hope it was worth it because you breached your own contract by crossing a clear line that I asked you not to. So whatever this was, it's over. I will finish the cases I am currently working on, and then I quit."

He took another sip of his drink before glancing over at me.

"This isn't about me crossing a line. It's about your fear of getting too close to me." He reached for something on the table in front of him and for the first time, I noticed the small, white envelope. "Give this to your mom," he said.

I walked over and took it.

"What is it?"

"It's a goodbye letter from Gary. I couldn't have him disappear and not give your mother at least an apology and some closure."

I was an idiot to walk out on this man. I knew it and he knew it, but pride could be a destructive thing, and all of my life, it was also the one thing that I always had lots of.

I left without another word and Merrick didn't try to stop me.

Chapter Sixteen

"I WAS TOO YOUNG TO DIE."

The next couple of weeks were work-filled and Merrick-free, resulting in... boring as hell. I'd be lying to myself if I said I didn't miss him, but I needed the time apart to sort myself out.

I was able to completely avoid Merrick because aside from going to the courthouse to battle cases, I'd been working from home. I turned in my two weeks resignation to Ashton and he took it.

Ashton didn't address the elephant in the room, no doubt Merrick had already made him aware of the circumstances, but he did say that he enjoyed working with me and wished me luck on all my future endeavors.

My response mirrored his sentiments, I loved my time at Dual and Ashton and Merrick were the best bosses I'd ever had.

"I love you and I respect you, but I will always cross the line if it means protecting you."

Merrick's words the last day I saw him replayed in my head, wearing on me, infuriating me, scaring me.

How could I trust him again? And if he did care about me, how did I handle that?

*Yes, m*en had told me they'd loved me before, but never,

not even once, had I ever felt the same. For all of my life, I had escaped these feelings. Now, I felt like cupid had me cornered, shooting me nonstop with arrows of love.

It was a Thursday night, and Jada and I were hanging out at my place. I worked from sun up to sundown, trying to finish all my cases, but since I had been doing it from home, my day-to-day had become quite isolating.

One day last week, I even admitted that I missed Amber, and if that wasn't a cry for help, I don't know what was.

Being a great friend, Jada came over to keep me company. Currently, we were doing nothing more than relaxing on my sofa.

My computer rested on my lap and files were stacked in a crooked pile beside the couch. Jada was next to me, flipping through a magazine, shoving a picture of a cute dress or fun hairstyle in my face every so often.

The goal was to pretend like everything was normal and I was holding up my end, but Jada kept stealing glances at me, waiting for an opportune moment to talk.

"Still thinking about him, huh?" Jada asked.

Looks like the opportune moment is now upon me.

"No," I said. My fingers glided across the keyboard at the 75 wpm speed I worked endlessly to accomplish. "I'm thinking about work. I have five accounts to close tonight, my final court case for Theodore Blakey tomorrow, then I am officially no longer a Dual employee."

"Is that what you really want? I thought you loved working for Dual."

"I do, but it's for the best."

Jada lowered her magazine. I noticed she had a finger inside holding her spot, so maybe this little talk wouldn't take long.

"Jocelyn, what are you really mad about here?"

"I told you, Jada. If Merrick can't respect my boundaries, that's a major issue. If I ignore what he has done, I am simply opening the doorway to him not respecting me at all, and then..."

"And then he'll become Gary and you'll become your mom?" Jada finished, her brow lifted in question. "Do you honestly think that is who Merrick is? Gary, in hiding? Or are you just looking for a reason to stop this before it goes too far because you're afraid?"

I rolled my eyes and clicked on a new email.

"Ugh, you sound just like Merrick."

Jada studied me, her hesitance indicating she was battling between holding back what she was thinking or setting it free. She went with free.

"I'm your best friend, so I'm just going to say it. This is stupid. Does it matter who got rid of Gary? Isn't the point that he is gone? You have been trying all these years to no avail. So what if Merrick stepped up to protect you, and your mom, might I add? You owe him your gratitude. Not to be cut out of your life."

Her words made sense. I didn't plan to cut him from my life... or maybe I did.

I couldn't think straight. Navigating the fluctuating emotions of romance was exhausting. Thanks to my inexperience, all I knew how to do was dissect it from a rational standpoint.

When you fell in love with someone, you were supposed to trust them. Did I trust Merrick? Is wanting to protect me a sufficient reason for butting in? Or is standing up for their woman just what men did and there was no getting around it? This was a headache.

I understand law, not love.

I thought about my mom and happiness filled my heart.

Her health was good and with Gary out of the picture, it was time for a change. She was going to sell her house and move into the senior citizen community with her friends.

I could see it now. There would be lots of bingo in her future.

To my utter amazement, my mom wasn't as broken up about Gary's parting as I thought she would be, especially after reading the letter Merrick forced Gary to write.

Apparently, in the note, Gary admitted and apologized for hitting me. Turns out that was my mom's line in the sand. She said that hurting her was one thing, but hurting me was another.

I still hadn't figured out if she stayed with him out of love or obligation, but now that he was gone, she wasted no time moving on.

I guess sometimes we need others to do the things we aren't strong enough to do for ourselves.

We'd rather remain in our own personal hells with the demons we know, than take the risk of running into those we don't, forgetting the whole time that there are angels out there as well.

It was becoming more and more clear to me that my problem was my fear of the unknown and my ego. It hurt me that Merrick was able to waltz into my life and solve a problem that I had been tackling for years with no success. I thought that I didn't need anyone, and now, I knew I was wrong.

I looked at Jada.

"I agree with you. I am a scared little girl with ego issues. There, I said it! Happy now?"

"I'd be much happier if you faced it."

My fingers paused on the keyboard.

"Honestly isn't my evident psychosis more of a reason that I should leave this whole thing alone? I am a wreck and I don't know if I'm coming or going. That is also why I could never be in a real relationship."

"But you were already in a relationship with Merrick," Jada said as if I were clueless.

"That was not a relationship. That was—"

"If you say that was the contract, I am going to shake you!"

She narrowed her eyes at me and I narrowed mine back.

"Fine," she said. "Looks like it's time for a CRD."

I grunted. CRD stood for Courtroom Debate. Jada and I did these mini-debate sessions when we felt the need to have a conversation on a lawyer-to-lawyer level, to prove that the other was being an idiot.

"One," Jada said. "You guys had sex exclusively with each other."

"The contract," I said, then ducked to avoid being hit with the pillow she threw at me.

These CRDs were not always professional.

Jada held up a second finger. "The dinners."

I wasn't budging on this. I crossed my arms and lifted my chin in defiance. "Still, part of the contract."

"Zip it!" Jada growled, holding up a third finger. "The trip to Paris."

"That was...," I tried to find an excuse, "a pity outing to make me feel better."

"To fucking Paris!" Jada exclaimed.

I facepalmed, the imaginary jury and I recognized when the truth was unavoidable.

Jada's voice softened. "And all those late nights where you talked to him about all the troubles of your heart?"

I scowled at her. "You get on my nerves."

She flipped her magazine back open and gave me a victorious smile. "That just means I won my case."

Merrick had me tied to his bed, completely naked and wearing my favorite nipple clamps. He lifted the small chain that connected the two clamps and pulled upward. I moaned, embracing the sweet pain the tension caused on my breasts.

"Open your mouth," Merrick said. I obeyed and he placed the chain on my tongue. "Close your mouth and keep the chain there. I want to make your nipples nice and sensitive for when I am playing with them later."

It felt like I only blinked and he was inside me, our bodies moving in slow motion as we communicated only using our minds.

"How are we speaking to each other without talking?" I asked him.

"Because you finally let me in. I'm in your head and your heart and I will always be there," he answered.

Everything started unfolding at rapid speed. He'd literally just entered me and now my toe-curling climax was closing in. I panicked. My eyes went wide and my mind formed the question that Merrick answered before I could even finish thinking it.

"If you ask for permission to cum then the chain will fall from your mouth. Do not drop the chain, Jocelyn."

"But... I don't know if I can... hold back."

I tried, I really did, but there was no halting that train. I came in a rush, the chain still in my mouth, my body spasming uncontrollably and one thought playing on repeat in my mind as I came undone.

Merrick smiled down at me and said, "It's okay, beautiful, I already know. I love you, too."

I woke from the dream in a snap, my hand in between my legs and my cell vibrating on the nightstand. I instantly got happy because I thought it was Merrick, but it wasn't. Nevertheless, the name on my display screen was shocking.

"Aaron," I said into the phone, checking the time.

"Jocelyn! I'm so glad you answered. How are you?"

His voice was loud and much too enthusiastic. He was drunk.

I sat up, my body tingling and shaking from the dream. I heard music in the background. *Was he at a party?*

"I'm fine, Aaron. Do you know it's after midnight? Where are you?"

"I'm with some friends and I know it's late, but I missed you. All the fun we had, the great conversations and... the sex," he added in a whisper, or his version of a whisper because it only sounded like he was speaking at a normal volume instead of shouting.

I couldn't help but laugh.

"The conversations were great," I admitted.

I wouldn't comment on the sex because what Aaron and I had was lightyears behind what I shared with Merrick. I moved the phone a few inches from my ear before I ended up with a ruptured ear drum.

"Good!" Aaron said. "That means maybe there is still a chance for us."

I twisted my fingers in the bedsheets, wishing I could avoid hurting him... again.

"No, Aaron, that ship has sailed. There will never be a chance for us."

"You said that last time, but I love you, Jocelyn, don't you get that?"

I fell back onto the pillow and laid my arm across my eyes in annoyance. Cupid was attacking everyone tonight.

"You think you love me, Aaron, but you couldn't because you don't even know me."

Hell, I barely knew myself, I wanted to add. Here it was I

thought that my world was structurally sound, turns out I'm an emotional wreck.

Aaron wasn't giving up.

"Is it something I did? Something I said? I can change, Jocelyn."

His despair tugged at my heart. The last time we spoke about this it turned into an argument. Aaron said things out of anger and so did I. Yet, right now, he was laying his heart on the table, and unfortunately, I had to smash it.

"Aaron, you are a great guy. Don't change yourself for anyone. There is a woman out there for you."

"But it's not you," he said, finally mastering a whisper. I didn't say anything. I'd given him enough rejection to get the point. He began to speak again. "Before I let you go, can you answer one question for me? It may sound weird, but please tell me there is at least someone else. I'd feel pretty pathetic if you're saying no because you'd prefer to be alone than with me."

I smiled, happy to give Aaron some good news. There was a man, a magnificent man, and I was in love with him. As soon as I finished my case tomorrow I was going to go get him.

"You know what, Aaron? There actually is... his name is Merrick."

It was early Friday morning and the courthouse was crowded, which was odd. Typically Mondays are the busiest due to all the people arrested over the weekend. As the week moves along, the flood of activity tends to taper down.

Thankfully, I always showed up an hour early. It gave me time to read the mood of the judge and jury, check notes and discuss any last-minute changes with the paralegal.

Although today I had no paralegal because Janie was with her son.

I entered the courtroom and took a seat on the right side where the Plaintiffs sat. A glance around the courtroom confirmed that Theodore Blakey wasn't here, but since it was still very early, I didn't expect he would be.

I opened my briefcase and began checking all evidence and supporting documents necessary for this case.

This was my fourth time, and my findings were the same as the last three – everything I needed was here and Janie had done a terrific job. I would miss her.

More people were pouring into the courtroom, taking their seats, so I closed my briefcase and straightened it on my lap. The judge would likely begin in the next few minutes.

Someone sat down in the chair next to me, which I vaguely thought was odd since there were quite a few chairs on this side of the courtroom available.

Either way, I was so lost in my own world that I didn't look over to see who it was, but when he said, "We meet again, Ms. Milner," my world stopped.

My heart skipped several beats. The man of my literal dreams was sitting next to me. His handsome face, chiseled jawline, perfect skin, and disarming dimples had my voice in a chokehold.

Don't you dare show signs that you need this man like you need your next breath, I threatened my heart to keep it in line.

Merrick brought a longing out of me that I didn't think I was capable of. My insides were on fire for him, but on the outside, I had to keep a neutral front.

"Merrick, what are you doing here?"

The irony was not lost on me that we were back where we started. Running into each other at the courthouse. Although this time, I was certain our meeting was not by accident.

"You know there was no way I would miss your last day working for Dual. After this case is over, we are going to spend the rest of the day together."

His words were like music to my ears, but my response was delayed. I was still taking all of him in. I couldn't believe he was here. Had my wet dreams from last night manifested the real thing?

Alright! Enough of that, I thought, silencing my body's shameless desires and fixing my eyes straight ahead.

"Don't you have meetings and such to attend?" I asked.

"Canceled them all. I'm here as your backup."

"How so?" I asked, intrigued.

"Janie couldn't make it, so I'll take notes for you."

My lips twitched at the corners. I loved our banter. It was like foreplay and I was relieved that after two weeks apart, we fell back into step so easily.

"That's cute," I said, "but you're not a paralegal."

"Alright then, I'm here to watch my lawyer represent my company."

"After today, I won't be your lawyer, remember? What else you got?"

"You," Merrick replied, his eyes so assertive, so captivating that my mouth fell slightly open. He placed his arm on the back of my chair and leaned close to my ear. "And later, when I have you tied to my desk and I'm eating your pussy to a point that you can barely breathe. Remember that you brought it on yourself."

I had to put my briefcase on the floor so that I could cross my legs. I swiped a loose curl from my forehead and straightened my shirt. Suddenly I felt very, very dirty...

"Yes, sir," I said with a wink.

That was all Merrick needed. He faced forward and we both waited in silence as the judge entered the courtroom and the cases began.

For the next hour, I watched case after case be decided. Most were in favor of the plaintiff, which I found reassuring and hopefully foretelling.

Nevertheless, the possibility that my case may close with a breeze wasn't the reason my spirit was happy and the room seemed brighter. That was all Merrick.

My peripheral view was working overtime, watching him and conjuring up naughty scenes that would consume my evening.

Twenty minutes before my case was up, Theodore entered the room and sat on the left side with the other defendants. He gave me a cold glare, no doubt blaming me for this mess he was in, but when Theodore glimpsed Merrick beside me, staring daggers at him, I could tell he almost shit his pants.

I laughed to myself, then mentally began rehearsing major points for my case. With this being my last one for Dual, I wanted to make them proud.

My time had arrived... well almost. Dual vs. Theodore Blakey was next in line. All I had to do was wait for a ruling on the case currently being presented and we were up.

However, that case was not going as smoothly as the others. Most people had taken their losses today and were off somewhere licking their wounds, but this guy was looking to inflict new ones.

His name was Dale Gladstone, and like Theodore, he was being sued for insurance fraud. The man prosecuting him, Zack Thatcher, sat at a table in front of me.

Dale kept speaking out of turn and paying no regard to not only the warnings given by his legal counsel but the judge as well.

"I didn't do shit," Dale screamed. "That suit-wearing motherfucker over there is lying on me."

Zack looked positively frightened and Dale snorted a laugh.

He was definitely a wild one and the honorable Judge Gail Walker looked like she was two seconds away from doing some dishonorable things. And not the kind that I wanted to do with Merrick.

Her lips were in a tight line, her nostrils were flared, and the arm of her robe shook vehemently as she slammed the gavel down several times.

"Counsel," Judge Gail said, "you settle Mr. Gladstone down before he is held in contempt. I will not give another warning."

"Fuck you!" Dale spat. "I'm not afraid of you."

I knew what would happen next. Dale was going to jail.

"Get him out of my courtroom, now!" Judge Walker shouted.

The woman was furious. I thought that if the bailiff didn't get to Dale fast enough, she would come down and cuff him herself.

Meanwhile, Dale was going crazy, kicking, screaming and swearing. It took two people to try and contain him and they weren't having much luck.

An odd thing happened next and I felt the hairs on the back of my neck stand. Something wasn't right. The way Dale was twisting out of their grasp seemed like he wasn't merely trying to get free, he had a more menacing goal in mind.

The Bailiff grabbed one of Dale's arms, but the man assisting wasn't quick enough to get the other. Dale yanked hard forward and got loose. Next, he faked left, actually turned right, and pressed up close to the bailiff, locking his fingers around the man's gun.

I have no idea how he got it out so fast. I thought they

were supposed to be strapped down, but none of that mattered now.

The courtroom broke out in a frenzy as Dale aimed the gun at Zack. My breath caught in my chest, not only for Zack's life but for my own. I was positioned behind Zack and that put me in the direct line of fire.

I needed to move, duck or run away, I was too young to die, too happy, and too in love, but once Dale pulled that trigger, I was too late.

Chapter Seventeen

"IS IT GOING TO HURT?"

I squeezed my eyes shut, a coldness covering my back and a weight on my chest.

Had I been shot? Was I going into cardiac arrest?

I was certain that my demise was in progress when the weight on my chest lessened, giving me the courage to look down.

Merrick was partially on top of me, his sleeve torn near the shoulder area and saturated with blood.

"Merrick! Merrick!" I said, shaking him hard, but he didn't respond.

No, this couldn't be happening. This is all a bad dream, just a bad dream.

Buried beneath part of his body, I strained my neck to search for help, but there was none. Panic swarmed around me, screams pierced my ears, and people clutched onto one another, hiding for their safety.

I glanced down again, pushing with all my strength to roll Merrick to his side. I caressed his face, my hands unsteady.

He was breathing... *so why wouldn't he respond? What was wrong? I had just got him again, I couldn't lose him!*

"You can't leave me like this, do you hear me? I love you. You can't leave me."

A tear rolled down my cheek and I gripped his uninjured arm, shaking him again. Probably not the smartest thing, but at the moment it was all I could think to do.

"Wake up! Wake up!"

There was sudden, slow movement as Merrick shifted in my arms, a weak smile spread across his face. "I knew you loved me," he said.

I was consumed with relief, and the terror clutching my heart eased.

The commotion in front of the court calmed. Dale was cuffed and carried out, angry as ever but no longer a threat.

People cautiously peeked around and over chairs, ensuring the coast was clear. I looked down at Merrick. The man I loved had saved my life for the second time.

"Are you okay?" I asked.

His head rested in my lap and I carefully checked his arm. Blood had stained his shirt, but the spot hadn't grown any larger.

"I'm fine," he said with a grunt, sitting up.

"But there's blood."

Merrick glanced at his arm.

"I think the bullet only grazed me, but I have the worst headache."

I studied my surroundings. A few people were still getting off the floor, clutching their arms, legs and head. Chairs and benches were out of place and flipped over all around the courtroom. Even the table that Zack was originally sitting at was turned over, its four wooden legs in the air.

It was likely in all the commotion that Merrick hit his head.

Trying to save me, I thought to myself.

"You got hurt protecting me," I said guiltily.

"I told you, I will always protect you."

I inspected his head and saw no knots or bruises and best of all, no blood.

"No damages that I can see," I said, "but you should still get checked out."

"Lucky for me, I have a hard head," Merrick said, able to make light of such a dark situation. "I guess it's a side effect of being so stubborn."

I placed both of my hands on his face and gently touched my forehead to his.

"Your stubbornness is what I love most about you."

We kissed, right there in the courtroom, not giving a damn about the laws we could be breaking or who saw us. We were not only alive, we were together, and right now, that was all that mattered.

Paramedics arrived to assess everyone. Thankfully, besides a few sprains and scratches, everyone was fine.

They cleaned up Merrick's cut, which required nothing more than a bandaid and checked his head. Everything looked good. Merrick had no concussion and was given the green light to go about his day.

The judge postponed the rest of the cases until late next week and everyone was dismissed.

Merrick's original plan was to take me out on the town and spoil me with food, shopping and spa treatments before returning to his place to enjoy the rest of our evening.

After the day we had, skipping to the end sounded heavenly.

We ordered lunch from a local vegan restaurant near Merrick's house and ate it while drinking wine and watching a movie. It was my first time trying a vegan restaurant, but it would not be the last. The meal I had put some of my favorite meat dishes to shame.

The conversation mostly consisted of the insane events of

the day, which meant any deep discussion about our time apart could wait until another. I was just happy to be alive. However, there was one thing that I'd wanted to know for a while now.

"May I ask you a question?" I said after taking the last bite of my butternut squash risotto.

"Whatever you'd like," Merrick replied.

"Of all the women you could have chosen to fall for, why me?"

He put down his fork and studied me.

"The fact that you ask me that is one of the reasons in itself."

I dabbed at my lips with a napkin, slightly sad that the meal was over. It was flavorful and filling. Definitely worth adding to my meal rotation.

"I don't follow," I said.

"Jocelyn, you are an incredible woman through and through and you don't even know it. I see your strength, you're ambitions and your compassion. Most women see me and they are attracted to my looks and money. Their goal is to get close to me for all the wrong reasons, but you... you're different. You aren't a taker, you are a giver, and I have never met someone more amazing to give my all to."

Dammit! Why does he pull at my heartstrings like this?!

My eyes glistened, and I pretended something was in them, but it didn't work. Merrick laughed at me and shook his head.

"You could have just said, you're a cool chick, Jocelyn," I teased, imitating his voice. "You didn't have to make me want to cry."

"Well, Jocelyn, you are a cool chick... *my* cool chick," Merrick said with enough seduction that my clothes almost took themselves off.

We resumed watching the movie while finishing our wine.

I sat up and stood, moving forward with my knees turned slightly inward to keep the balls in.

Merrick thought my walk was hilarious.

"What are you doing?" he asked.

"I don't want them to fall out!"

"They are not going to fall out."

"Are you sure?" I asked, straightening my legs. "I want to make you proud, but they are putting some pretty serious weight on my entrance."

"Your desire to please me is expected and appreciated, but trust me, they aren't going anywhere."

Merrick grabbed my hand and I took a step, then another and another. I was beginning to feel confident and free until... it happened.

The balls rubbed together inside me and a strong sensation of pleasure came forth.

I gripped the stair rail to brace myself. "Woah!"

Merrick gave me a knowing smile. "Good, they're working."

If by working, Merrick meant that Ben was making himself delightfully known every few steps, then he was correct.

By the time I got out of the shower, I could barely walk more than several steps before I had to pause to get my quivering in order.

Goodness! Merrick said it would heighten my sensations, not send me to space.

The sporadic delightful tingles had become very deliberate in toying with my pussy.

Thanks to Merrick, and his need to run his soapy fingers over my erogenous zones repeatedly in the shower, I'd already had one orgasm and now I wanted another.

The problem was that Ben was great at building the need

but horrible at giving me the actual release. I required direct stimulation to my clit to set another orgasm free.

Therefore, I was stuck in orgasmic limbo with these brutal balls performing an edging game on me.

"I think... I need... to sit down, sir," I said, placing my hand on the wall, another wave of powerful pleasure rolling in.

We were in the hallway on the way back downstairs. To go where? I had no clue, but I hoped we got there fast. I wanted to sit down. I'd had the balls in for close to an hour and every shift of my hips or step I took was teasing me.

"When you get to my office, you can sit down for as long as you want."

Why did we need to go to his office?! He could have me right here! Right now, on the floor! Rug burn be damned.

I was only wearing a towel and with all the starting, stopping, bending and straightening I was doing it kept falling. Eventually, Merrick yanked it off and abandoned it on the stairs.

With those damn balls clicking and clacking in my pussy the entire way, we finally made it to Merrick's office.

He picked me up and placed me on top of his desk, cuffing my hands behind me then securing those cuffs to the desk. He had me lean forward to ensure that I was restrained to his liking before he began.

Taking a seat in his office chair, Merrick spread my legs wide, placing one foot on either armrest.

Merrick teased my earlobes, neck, and breasts with his hands, lips and tongue before moving toward the main event. I was much too eager, arching forward and wiggling my hips to get closer to his mouth.

"Calm down, Jocelyn." Merrick smirked, sitting back in his chair. "When I first saw you in the courtroom today, you fought so hard not to give into how badly you wanted me, now look at you, falling apart at just the thought of my touch."

The man wasn't lying, but how dare he use my vulnerable state of arousal against me! He better be glad I was tied to this desk or I'd push him to the floor and sit on his face. I opened my mouth to tell him just that...

"I'm sorry, sir. I was out of line."

Dammit! I was ready to tell him off, but my aching body made me putty in his hands.

Merrick smiled.

"I'm not convinced," he said.

I tried again. My hand squeezed into fists behind my back, my body on fire with need.

"Please, sir."

"Please, what?" Merrick asked cooly, resting his face against his open hand.

"Please eat my pussy, sir."

"Why?"

"Because I want it so bad, I want *you* so bad," I practically panted.

He considered it.

"What about your behavior earlier?"

"I was wrong, sir. Wrong to pretend that I didn't need you and wrong not to tell you how much I love you."

Merrick sat forward. A look of satisfaction spread across that gorgeous face.

"Was that so hard, beautiful?"

I shook my head.

Pointing a finger at me, he said, "Keep your legs open, or I will restrain them as well. I am expecting a call shortly, let's see how many orgasms I can get from you while we wait."

Four. The magical number was four.

I had what felt like one tsunami-level orgasm, followed by

a series of mini ones that had me seizing the armrest with my toes, fighting to keep my legs spread.

I was hyperventilating.

The added stimulation from the balls pinging together inside me made me plead for more and beg for less simultaneously.

Then, Merrick decided to alternate between tapping the toys with his tongue and sucking the life out of my clit, so I guess I was going to have that heart attack from earlier when I thought Dale had shot me after all.

Merrick did say he would have me tied to his desk and barely able to breathe, I thought. *The man always followed through on his promises.*

The balls shifted inside me and I gasped.

"It feels... so intense, sir. Are you... going to take the balls out soon?" I questioned, needing a break from the soul-shaking orgasms these balls, combined with his skills, were inducing.

"With how easily it's making you cum and how good you taste," Merrick said before dragging his tongue over my opening and then up to my clit, "not a fucking chance."

His desk phone rang, and without looking at it, he hit a button and paused long enough from licking me senseless to say one word. "Yeah."

"I got the final numbers from the three deals we closed with Built Tin. Are you ready for them?"

It was Ashton, and as usual, he was all business.

"Go ahead," Merrick replied before diving back in.

It was a simple response, but unlike the first time, he didn't move back as far from my sweet spot before answering. The way his voice vibrated through me carried a pulsating punch to my pussy. I sucked in a breath and bit down on my bottom lip to keep quiet.

Ashton began speaking. "7 million..." *oh shit,* I

thought, *I'm about to cum again.* "13.4 million," *yes, keep going!* "and 22 million."

I came again. It was out of my control.

I wasn't a gold digger, but in my defense, having a man that made that type of money on the regular with his face buried between my legs was its own aphrodisiac.

"We have two more deals closing next week from the clients you met in Miami. I will let you know when the numbers come in," Ashton said.

Merrick paused from licking circles around my clit.

"Good deal. Thanks for the info."

"Of course," Ashton said. "Oh, and bye, Jocelyn."

The call ended and I screamed. I attempted to pull my hands forward, intending to cover my face from embarrassment but forgot they were tied behind me. Merrick thought my predicament was amusing.

"No need to be embarrassed. Ashton knows you're mine."

Rising from his chair, Merrick wiped his mouth before placing one hand flat against my pussy and massaging it.

"YESSSS," I cried. The balls shifted forcefully inside, making my walls light up in pleasure like a pinball machine.

Merrick yanked on the tiny string and the balls ejected. A new, highly sensitive sensation caused me to try and snap my legs shut, but Merrick blocked it.

"Now, here comes the fun part," he said.

Ripping his towel from his waist, he dragged me closer to the edge of the desk and sheathed his dick into my center. I was not ready for sensitivity of this magnitude. I put the heel of my foot on the edge of his desk and tried to push my body back to get away, but Merrick only held me tighter.

I felt pleasure in my ass, thighs, back and toes. I begged, incoherently, for Merrick to give me a break so that I could at least regain some decency. The man had me no longer speaking English!

Was this a side effect of Ben?

Jada better watch out, I'd found a new pocket-sized best friend.

Time seemed to stand still as I took all that Merrick had to give. I was weak and the only reason I was sitting upright was because Merrick's arms were wrapped around my body, holding me still as he dug deep.

"I love you," he whispered, his lips pressed against my forehead as his dick so savagely and so erotically took me apart.

Epilogue

"IT'S YOUR ASS
NOW, SIR."

✤

I stared at the picture of my mom, dad, and I at a lake house we used to rent during the summers. In the photo, my dad had one arm around me and the other around my mom, his 'rays of sunshine' he would call us.

He was kissing my mom on the cheek while she and I made funny faces at the camera.

They were so in love. It was one of my favorite photos of the three of us and she'd found the perfect place to hang it.

Turning around, I watched Merrick and my mom sitting at the kitchen table, laughing like they were lifelong friends. If my suspicions were correct, she was sharing yet another story about something wild I did as a kid.

I came here once a week to visit her in her new home – a fabulously cozy senior citizen community. If business permitted, Merrick came with me and those two always acted the same.

Feigning annoyance, I rolled my eyes and shook my head as the two of them shared another laugh, but truth be told, I loved how easily they connected.

Since becoming an adult, I had never brought a man home. This was the first time my mom could share the stories about raising her rambunctious, headstrong daughter, and I wouldn't take that away from her.

"What are you two talking about now?" I said. "It better not involve me."

My mom waved me off. "Nothing like that this time. Come on, sit!" she urged, patting a seat for me to join them. Merrick stood and pulled it out for me, ever the gentleman. "We were talking about Janice Dorsey. She's my neighbor from two doors down and always looks so put together. Anyway, yesterday we had a water aerobics class and her wig came off. At first, no one knew it was a wig. We all thought a rat had jumped in with us. Imagine twenty or more seniors slipping and sliding all over the place, trying to get out of that pool."

My mom began laughing again, and I couldn't help but join in. It wasn't just the story, it was her smile, her animated hand movements and her spirit. She was truly happy here.

Merrick's cell rang and he excused himself, stepping out on the patio to take the call.

"You really love him, don't you?" my mom asked, watching me watch him.

"I do."

She squeezed my hand.

"Love is such a wonderful thing. I am so glad you allowed yourself to experience it," then leaning in, she whispered, "What he feels for you is real."

If there were any doubt in my mind about choosing to follow my heart when it came to Merrick, that would have sealed it. Despite her poor judgment when it came to Gary, I trusted my mom.

I squeezed her hand back and glanced around.

"This place fits you perfectly, mom. After being here for almost six months, do you still love it?"

"More than ever!" she said, her eyes lighting up. "Between the exercise classes, bingo, movie nights and various meetup groups... my calendar stays full. And the best part is I can do it all without leaving the community."

Over the past year, my mom kept her driving to a minimum. She said that all the cars on the road made her nervous which meant that her new home offered another major perk.

I snapped my fingers, "That reminds me. Won any cool bingo prizes lately?"

That got her talking for the next hour straight. From bingo, she moved on to poker night, then to how much she loved taco Tuesdays, but when the lady in 3B volunteered in the kitchen, my mom preferred to make her own food because, according to her, that lady never washed her hands.

My mom was a ball of entertainment and I cherished our time together. Before leaving, Merrick promised that next time we would take her somewhere special just to give her a change of scenery.

Once we returned to his place, I settled in at the kitchen island to get some work done. We had reservations for dinner in a few hours and I wanted to finish my summation for a new case I was working on to ease Mr. Hill's anxiety.

Gregory Hill was my new boss at a small pharmaceutical company I signed on to work for five months ago. Although I'd never lost a case since starting there, the possibility of losing any money made the man sweat bullets.

Therefore, I always gave him a brief run-through of my planned summation to soothe his unease.

The extra step may have been a headache to another lawyer, but I felt it better prepared me for presenting my case to the judge and jury.

Nevertheless, I did miss Dual sometimes.

Shortly after I closed and won the case against Theodore Blakey, I left the company. It wasn't because I was being petty, trying to teach Merrick a lesson, or didn't believe I could work beside him. I left Dual for me.

From the first day I met him, vulgar fucking aside, he'd treated me with nothing but the utmost respect. However, in the end, I think not working under him gave me the balance to satisfy my extreme need for independence.

Merrick was nothing short of super supportive and didn't once make me feel guilty about my decision to leave.

"Jocelyn," Merrick called from the bedroom, aka the kinky corner, renamed by yours truly. "can you come here for a second?"

I typed a few more words on my laptop, grinning like crazy, before closing it and heading to the room. The only time he called me in there was when he was ready for my obedience.

Entering the room, I immediately noticed the dim lighting and Merrick standing by the long thick rope that hung from the ceiling. He was wearing his usual casual clothes, jeans, and a t-shirt, but the look in his eyes promised me that whatever he had planned would be epic and wild.

A few months ago, I asked Merrick if we could introduce more extreme kinks in our Dom/sub relationship, but Merrick hadn't agreed. He said when the time was right he would give me what I'd been hoping for. Maybe tonight was the night.

"Yes, sir," I said, approaching him.

"There is something new I want to try with you," he said.

Oh yeah, I am about to get fucked to a whole new level and I can't wait.

"Of course. What do you need me to do?"

Merrick directed me toward the rope, having me hold onto it with both hands, putting me back in the Eiffel tower position. The only difference was this time, I was clothed, which meant he was about to do something extreme.

I hope he is going to rip my clothes off, I thought. Getting myself hot and bothered before we even officially got going.

"Now," he said assertively, "not letting go of the rope, I want you to get on your knees."

"Yes, sir."

I began lowering myself, pulling the rope with me, but it barely moved. I tried a second time and got the same result."

"What's wrong?" Merrick asked.

"The rope is stuck."

"Pull harder," he ordered.

"Yes, sir," I yanked with all my strength and the rope finally gave way.

What I saw next left me speechless.

Suddenly lights shone in various spots throughout the room, giving it an enchanting glow.

Then all around me, fragrantly-scented rose petals, balloons, and tiny gold stars fell from the ceiling, showering me like a princess in a fairy tale.

I spun around in a slow circle, pure bliss holding me captive. There must have been hundreds of petals and stars falling all around me. They landed at my feet, on my clothes, and in my hair, blanketing the floor as the romance rained down.

It was so incredibly beautiful that only one word could describe this scene, magical.

When my eyes returned to Merrick, he was on one knee, holding open a black velvet box that contained one of the most breathtaking rings I'd ever laid eyes on.

"Will you marry me, Jocelyn?"

My hand flew to my mouth and I shook my head frantically.

It wasn't that I was saying no, I simply couldn't believe this was happening. Realizing that Merrick may have thought, "no" was my answer. I shouted, "Yes!" and ran to him, almost knocking him over.

He steadied us easily and flipped me over to my back, where I melted into a soft, colorful pile of roses and stars.

"You have made me the happiest man alive," he said.

I touched his face and stared into his eyes. He was my everything.

Picking up one of the rose petals, I sniffed it. My eyes filled with tears.

Damn you, waterworks! Always making me look like a crybaby.

"You made roses beautiful and pure again," I whispered with a sniffle.

My unfavorable recollections concerning roses would be put to rest after this night, I was certain of it.

"No more bad memories, my love," Merrick said, wiping tears from my cheek. "you deserve all the happiness in the world and I will spend the rest of my life giving it to you."

I swallowed the lump in my throat and nodded. I couldn't trust myself to respond, the tears were coming much too fast and blurring my vision. I wiped at my eyes, attempting to pull myself together, but when Merrick kissed me, I threw in the towel.

I wrapped my arms around his neck as he carried me to the bed, laying me down like I was delicate glass that he feared would break.

Merrick undressed me using an arousing slowness that not only kept me in the moment but prolonged it, and for that, I was grateful. This was an experience I never wanted to forget.

Once he was done, we exchanged exploration roles as I undressed him, lifted his shirt, and unfastened his jeans, planting kisses and gentle nips all over his warm, smooth skin.

There was no Dom/sub dynamic, no bondage, no accessories, just two people putting their hearts on the line and being completely transparent with each other.

We laughed as loving words passed between our lips when heartfelt kisses weren't.

Merrick's tongue tasted every inch of me with a sensual tenderness that had more tears escaping. My heart was so full of love and passion that I couldn't tell if I was coming or going, but once Merrick finally pushed inside, connecting his body to mine, I knew I was home.

Lights flickered, casting shadows on the wall that were as in sync with their lovemaking as we were. I was his, he was mine and nothing else mattered.

Afterward, as a newly engaged, very late couple, we arrived at dinner, which turned out to be another surprise. It was an intimate engagement party, consisting of only the family and friends we both held near and dear.

I couldn't believe that my mom and Jada knew about the party for weeks and didn't tell me. Apparently, they were better at keeping exciting news than I was because they didn't give the slightest inkling that something was going on.

The celebration was beyond anything I could have asked for – speeches were given, toasts were made, the food and drinks were phenomenal and we partied all night.

"Very slick and a bit cocky, Mr. Alexander," I said, pulling him aside to get a quick moment alone. "Planning an engagement party before the actual proposal. How did you know I would say yes?"

"Because you can't resist me," was his conceited response. He drew me close and we began to slow dance. "But if that didn't work, I would have tied you up and made sweet love to you until you said yes."

"Hmm, is it too late to take that option? Because if it isn't, I want in on that." Merrick lifted my arm and twirled me around. Pulling my body up against his, he said, "your wish is always my command."

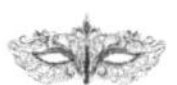

"Relax your shoulders, calm your breathing and I want you to try it again," Merrick said.

I did as told and let his voice soothe and guide me. I was on my knees blindfolded, wearing a collar that connected two clamps to my nipples and one to my clit.

These particular clamps were very cool because they were adjustable.

Depending on Merrick's mood, they could be set to give barely any pressure or so much that it was hard to concentrate on anything else. Call me crazy, but on the days he liked to push my limits, I loved how much the pain intensified my orgasms.

Today wasn't an intense day, which meant the clamps felt like my nipples and clit were only being lightly pinched.

Merrick was training me to deep-throat him for longer stretches because he loved the way his dick felt in my mouth, and so did I.

"Are you ready?" he asked.

"Yes, sir."

I opened my mouth and his dick filled it. I relaxed as he had instructed me to, and he began to count.

"One, two, three..." he looped a finger around the collar I was wearing and used it to pull me closer so that he was all the way in. "Eleven, twelve, thirteen, fourteen..."

My shoulders stiffened like they had the first time when I felt myself needing to take a breath and Merrick pulled out immediately. I gasped for air, the rush of endorphins and teasing pressure from the clamps making me eager to try again.

Merrick toyed with the collar.

"I like the way this looks on you. Maybe I should consider adding a leash to it."

"If that appeases you, sir," was my automatic reply.

He smiled down at me, my answer of submission not surprising him in the least.

At this point in our Dom/sub relationship, Merrick made all the decisions, and to date, he hadn't done a single thing that I didn't thoroughly enjoy.

From punishments to rewards and everything in between, we were in sync. Merrick was amazing at giving me balance. He knew my limits, my dislikes, and when I wanted our love-making to be naughty and nasty or intimate and romantic. I trusted him completely.

Removing the blindfold, he said, "You've done well today and earned your reward. Go ahead and finish. I'm ready to cum."

"Thank you, sir."

I licked my lips and wrapped my hand around his dick, holding him steady so I could get started. This was the part I craved, the actual sucking, and I couldn't wait for him to unload into my mouth.

My lips slid down his dick until I felt them touch my hand. I repeated the action several times, not stopping until his fingers twisted into my hair. Next, I removed my hand and swallowed his entire length, just the way he liked it.

"That's a good whore. Take it all in," he aggressively insisted, setting my body ablaze with the use of my favorite pet name.

I dragged my tongue over the head, alternating between making it firm or soft as I teased the tip. Once I incorporated some of the techniques he'd had me practicing while doing my throat contracting trick, he came hard, and I devoured every drop.

Once he was done using my mouth, Merrick instructed me to face away from him in the doggy-style position. Lifting me by my hips, he then tells me to grip his waist with my legs.

"This position is called the wheelbarrow, and it gives me a great view of your ass."

I giggled.

"It's your ass now, sir."

Merrick laughed and tightened his hands on my waist.

"I fucking love you," he said and thrust himself inside hard and fast.

I was immediately in the zone because this angle easily allowed his dick to rub against my G-spot. Flattening my palms on the floor, I pushed back every time he pushed forward, my legs trembling uncontrollably as my release rounded the corner.

Merrick reached out and adjusted the tightness of the clamp on my clit until I moaned loudly in satisfaction. After that, it took no time for my first orgasm to arrive on the scene.

I shook, yelled, and eventually, my upper half collapsed on the floor. I assumed since I was no longer doing my part to make our wheelbarrow position as effective that Merrick would stop, but I should have known he didn't need my help.

Without breaking a sweat, he used his skillful thrusts to wheel me to my climax over and over again.

The bubbles floated around Merrick and I as we relaxed in his 6-foot soaker tub. This was my second favorite spot in the house after the kinky corner.

Two glasses of wine sat nearby and soothing jazz played, creating the perfect ambiance.

I stared at the ring, my hand outstretched, still not believing it was there. I hadn't set a date yet, but that was because I needed time. We'd only been engaged for two months and already I had a to-do list a mile long.

I guess the younger version of me that wanted the whimsical fairytale wedding wasn't dead after all. She was only asleep, waiting for a kiss from her perfect prince.

"Do you want me to move in here after the wedding?" I asked.

Merrick kissed the back of my neck and began massaging my shoulders.

"That is totally up to you."

"Can we buy a new house on the lake?"

"Fine with me."

"Can we get married in the spring?"

"If that's what you want," he said, placing another kiss on my neck.

"The winter?" I asked suspiciously.

"If it makes you happy."

My hand dropped into the soapy water.

"The desert?!" I said flatly.

"It's different and will likely be very hot, but if that's what you want, it works for me."

"Merrick! Do you even care where we get married? How we get married? Or when we get married?"

He placed his hand around my waist and tugged me back onto his chest.

"I do not. As long as we *get* married, I am leaving all that up to you."

"So you have no requests?"

"Not really. All I need is you, at the altar, in your wedding dress." Merrick lifted my hand from the water and kissed it. "And now that I think about it, you don't even need the dress."

I picked up a hand full of bubbles and blindly tossed it behind me. I felt him shift to dodge it, and we shared a laugh.

"Only you would want me naked at our wedding."

"I want you happy, Jocelyn," he said. His voice was sincere and patient. Making my heart flutter and reminding me why I loved him so much. "I didn't forget all you shared with me about your perfect wedding or that you have a book stuffed with a million ideas. Your happiness is my only concern so go crazy, my love. You can have whatever you want."

I spun around and gave him a long passionate kiss.

"Thank you, Mr. Alexander," I said, gazing into his eyes. "I love you."

"I love you too, Mrs. Alexander," he replied.

I got goosebumps.

Facing forward, I began gathering up bubbles and gently blowing them away.

"How's Dual?"

I had to ask because Merrick never brought it up. I think he didn't want me to feel like he was trying to burden me with a job I had left behind. Nevertheless, I liked to make it known that I was there anytime he needed me, employee or not.

Merrick sighed and took a sip of his wine.

"We had to fire the lawyer we hired to replace you."

I stopped making my bubble mountain.

"Oh no! It took you and Ashton months to find her. I thought it would work out."

"So did I, but she couldn't handle the workload. She kept falling behind on cases."

"That sucks. Is there anything I can do?"

"No, we will figure something out. Besides, I'm starting to think Ashton wants the next lawyer he hires to be willing to serve more than just the legal position."

I spun around again.

"You mean Ashton is looking for a new mouthpiece?"

"Yup."

I thought about it, a grin spreading across my face as a thrilling, devious plan formed in my mind.

Jada is going to kill me for this, but I simply can not resist.

If you enjoyed this book, please leave me a five star review. It helps out so very much.

WANT MORE MERRICK & JOCELYN?

KEEP READING for a sneak peek of
Valentine's with a Dom: A Romantic, BDSM Novel

Valentine's WITH A DOM

—— BY NICKI GRACE ——

STARRING:

Merrick Alexander and Jocelyn Alexander

GUEST APPEARANCE BY:

Blaze

HIS MOUTHPIECE SERIES

SCENE 2
Caged

Merrick approached, tapping the top of the cage. The light clink made me wince, as it sent vibrations through the metal bars that aggravated my already sore limbs.

I'd been waiting so long that I became convinced he'd finished the movie and then started it again.

Even though I wished to give him a severe case of blue balls, I was happy to see him. He was just so damn alluring, with that face, body, and infuriating unbothered demeanor.

"I brought you something," he announced casually.

"Did you?" I replied steadily, ignoring my aching shoulders. "What is it?"

"I promised you roses," he stated, revealing a rose-shaped vibrator.

I chuckled and leaned my head back, too tired to hold it upright. "You said roses, which is plural," I announced, pointing out the discrepancy. "You're only holding one rose."

Apparently, I still wanted to be a brat, but Merrick didn't comment on it. Instead, he examined the pleasure device in his hand, turning it this way and that.

"Hmm, something tells me I'll only need one to get the job done."

Yup, I could see it in his eyes. He didn't comment because

he was also going to punish me for that remark. I decided it was in my best interest to stop being an ass for now. At least until I was out of this cage.

"Have you enjoyed being the center of attention?" he asked.

"It was eye-opening, Sir," I admitted, my tone polite.

"So you would say you learned your lesson?"

I nodded and spoke at the same time. "Yes, I did."

"Good, because this next part I think you will enjoy... well, sort of."

I stared up at him in confusion but remained silent, not trusting myself to speak.

Merrick removed his shirt, and even through the pain, I was so desperate for some action that my lips parted slightly, and I was practically salivating at the sight, like some damn eager puppy.

It made the fact that he had me locked in a cage fitting and highly comical.

He sat on the floor in front of the cage, facing me, his broad shoulders and sculpted chest rising and falling with each slow, measured breath.

The quiet strength in the way he held himself is almost disarming, like he's unshakeable, and I'm still trying to remember how to breathe correctly.

Sometimes I stared at him in complete disbelief that he's mine. This man could command a room with a single glance, and at this moment, that quiet power was directed entirely at me.

The intense eyes, the sharp line of his jaw, and the way the light swept across the muscles of his arms all hit me at once.

There's a flutter in my chest, a blend of desire and awe. I don't know if it's his physical appeal or the way he commands me, but every time I see him like this, it leaves me utterly undone.

The vibrator was beside him, and I realized the device resembled the one at home, featuring a dial that measured intensity from one to ten. I adored that toy; it was my favorite, yet I could never get beyond level four.

I attempted it once out of sheer curiosity, but by the time I reached level seven, I had curled my finger so tightly against the bed that I ended up breaking two nails.

Merrick reached through the cage opening, his fingers sliding along my inner thigh. The contact was barely a brush, but my eyes fluttered shut instantly, a soft sigh slipping from my lips.

It's ridiculous how easily he turned me into this. And he knew it.

Merrick's voice was gentle and serene when he spoke. "Open your eyes."

I obeyed, and he watched me with a quiet hunger that radiated curiosity rather than urgency. It's as if he wanted to absorb every detail, to commit this moment to memory.

His hand moved excruciatingly slowly up my thigh and toward my pussy. I didn't break eye contact, but as his hand drew closer, I inched forward, and he stopped.

A quick shake of his head reminded me to stay in my place, and my place is under his direction.

Frustration burned, and I was on edge, but I composed myself, breathed, and submitted to the command.

Only when I am motionless did he continue.

Tension coiled through me, and my breath lodged halfway in my throat. The moment his fingers brushed the edge of my sensitivity, a shiver rolled through me before I could restrain it.

"I see you are already wet," he said.

I nod.

Withdrawing his hand, Merrick picked up the vibrator. "What level do you normally use this on?" he asked.

"Four," I offered.

"Four?" he repeated, turning it over in his hand again. "But there are ten levels on here."

"True, but four is the highest level I can comfortably handle, Sir."

Merrick lowered the device. "Well, tonight let's get you up to ten."

The cloud of bliss vanished, and at his words, I think my pussy shrieked. There was no way in hell he was going to get me up to ten without sending me into a coma!

WANT TO KEEP READING?

Valentine's with a Dom is Available Now

USE THE QR CODE BELOW TO VISIT MY WEBSITE

<u>Romance</u>

The Inevitable Encounters Series

Book 1: The Hero of my Love Scene

Book 2: The Love of my Past, Present

Book 3 : The Right to my Wrong

The Love Is Series

Book 1: Love is Sweet

Book 2: Love is Sour

Book 3: Love is Salty

<u>Erotica</u>

His Mouthpiece

His Mouthpiece: The Prequel

This Side of Wrong - Coming soon

<u>Thrillers</u>

The Twisted Damsel

Break Him

Women's Fiction

Cut off Your Nose to Spite Your Face

The Splintered Doll (A Memoir)

Self-Help

The TIPSY COUNSELOR Series

The Tipsy Dating Counselor (Summary)

Book 1: The Tipsy Dating Counselor (UNRATED)

Book 2: The Tipsy Marriage Counselor

Book 3: The Pregnancy Counselor

About the Author

Nicki Grace is an Atlanta native with a bachelor's in business and a Masters in Marketing. As a wife, mother, author and designer, she is addicted to writing, spas, laughing, and sex jokes, but not exactly in that order.

Her comedic personality and unique upbringing by an illiterate but fiercely strong mother and a courageous, prideful father, made her view of the world pretty unconventional.

Luckily for you, someone gave her internet access, and now you get to experience all the EMOTIONAL, EXCITING, SHOCKING, and HOT ideas that reside in her head. She loves to have fun and lives for a good story. And we're guessing so do you! Nickigracenovels.com

facebook.com/nickigracenovels

instagram.com/nickigracenovels

tiktok.com/@nickigracenovels

bookbub.com/authors/nicki-grace